THE UNREAL

Kellyn Toombs

Additional copies of The Unreal
can be
purchased on Amazon or
Amazon Kindle

DEDICATION

To my grandparents

PROLOGUE

Ten years. That was how long it had been. Ten torturous, antagonizing, terrible years since they had died. And he had spent every single day of those ten years searching for them. Trying to find their spirits, trying to bring them back. He had never believed in the afterlife before, but he did now, if only because he needed to.

Ten years, and all his attempts at reaching them had been failures. This time, he would not fail.

This time, he had the real, actual, original copy of the Voynich Manuscript stolen from the special collections of Yale University.

This time, he had translated it, and translated it well; he was the first person ever to successfully understand the ancient forgotten language. He struggled to comprehend a few words, yes, and certain rules for conjugations and sentence structures always threw him off. But he couldn't stall from casting the spell any longer.

For this time, he had the corpse of a chupacabra, stolen from the New World museum.

This time, he had his blood and their bones.

This time, he cried.

Then, he turned out the lights, set everything aflame, started his chant, and prayed.

This time, something happened.

This time, something went wrong.

The glass of the windows shattered, the bones melted, the blood spilled onto the floor. He screamed and lay writhing on the ground as the mutant dog's corpse fell on top of him.

And then, the world lay still.

Something had happened. His face was not just his face anymore. He was in his office, his workspace at Area 51, but it was not as he had known it. He looked out the window, slowly, tentatively, and everything looked the same, but he wasn't in the real world anymore. He felt it, and he knew something was different. Something wasn't the same. He touched the left side of his face, the broken side, slowly becoming aware of what had gone wrong. He had meant to bring them to him in another level of reality. He had meant to chant, "Let us three be together in this layer for all of time." Though he wouldn't realize his mistake, through his errors with similar words and plurals within the ancient language, he had chanted, "Let us all in groups of three be combined in this layer over time."

The spell had only partially succeeded, but he could fix this. It would take time, but he could still search for them here. He stood, picked the mangled dog corpse off the floor, and held it in his arms for a moment. He was closer to them. He had made progress. He turned around, sniffing the air. He was going to find them. And with that, he walked out the door, looking at the sky of his newfound reality. The world had changed. He had changed. He could find them now.

That was five years ago.

CONCORD

I didn't really know what to do with myself.

There comes a point in the grieving process when you've cried enough that you can't cry anymore, but you aren't over your grief enough to go about your life, so you can't really bring yourself to be doing anything at all. This was the state I had reached. It was a week after my grandma had died, and yet here I was, still sitting beside her now not-quite-as-freshly-dug grave.

Opal M. Hewes
April 12, 1930 - June 2, 2015
Mother, Grandmother, Sister, Friend
Treasured Forever.

A simple cross etched at the bottom of the stone. I stared at the death date over, and over, and over. It was hard to put my mind around it. She was dead.

I'm normally a mild-mannered, happy person, but dealing with her death had been hard, to say the least. I'd sunken into a depressed, lifeless emotional state and struggled to see the good in anything. Grandma had always been there for me; the one person I trusted more than anyone. Living without Grandma meant living without someone to walk with me to church every Sunday morning, living without summer vacations to Cape Cod, living without someone to exchange hand-knitted mittens with every Christmas, living without someone to tell all my secrets to at the end of the day.

But one of the hardest things to deal with, beside losing my best friend and most trusted family member, was the fact that I would now be experiencing a change in custody. My parents had died in a car crash when I was six months old, so I had lived with my Grandma for almost all my life. She was the one who raised me, who packed my lunches and picked me up from school, who helped me with homework and took me shopping, who had taught me almost everything I knew about life. And now she was gone.

There was a cousin, of course, that I would be living with while I completed three more years of high school. She was older than me, with a husband and a daughter, but she didn't really talk to me much, and I was too terrified to start a conversation of my own. There was a room I could have in her house. It was small though, with no windows, and I was going to have to go to a new high school in Rhode Island. A public school.

I guess that's why I really couldn't bring myself to leave Grandma's grave. I was desperately clinging to the past, hoping that if I held on hard enough, the future would never come. I'd always had a problem with getting too attached to things. Grandma would have to remove the clothes in my closet that I'd outgrown in the middle of the night until I was ten. I still had my old baby blanket on the foot of my bed. But this change was different, more emotional, more severe. You can replace clothes and blankets. Nothing can replace a person.

I traced the cross on Grandma's grave with my finger. Died June 2, 2015. This wasn't real. This wasn't my life. Tomorrow, I'd wake up in our house on Smart Street, and Grandma would shuffle out of her bedroom at exactly 7:25 to start making breakfast. She'd kiss the top of my head, hand me a homemade muffin, and wish me luck on my science test.

What was actually going to happen was I would wake up in my house on Smart Street alone, and for the last time, before my cousin arrived with a stack of cardboard boxes to help me pack the last of my things. Then she'd drag me away to her horrid house in Providence where I'd make my own breakfast while struggling to keep it away from a greedy three-year-old and get on a gross and crowded yellow school bus without anyone saying goodbye or even knowing I had a science test. I would normally never say such a thing in front of Grandma, but honestly? It was going to suck. And I was terrified.

Now, all of this seems ordinary enough, right? I mean, most kids don't have two dead parents at the time in their life when they lose their grandma, and most kids aren't sent off to live with a cousin they aren't fond of in the slightest, but this sounds like something that could realistically happen. People die. People have to move. These are real-life, not extraordinary situations. But as for what happened to me next, let's just say it was different.

I wasn't really sure how it started. I still don't fully understand it now. I do know that before it happened, I was sitting on the ground hugging Grandma's tombstone, my head resting against the cold, hard granite. I remember staring at the grass in front of me, trying desperately to motivate myself to at least stand up. Then, everything changed.

DESERT

I couldn't tell you how it happened if I tried. One moment, I was sitting in the grass, clinging to a headstone in Oak Lawn Cemetery. The next, I was lying on a hot, sandy patch of ground, with nothing but more sand and the cloudless blue desert sky surrounding me for miles.

It took a moment for me to adjust from the shock and realize where I was, or more accurately, where I wasn't.

I pushed myself to my feet in a panic. How had I gotten here? Where *was* here? I could feel my breath and heart racing at the same pace as I whipped around to search every direction, looking for another person, a road, a building, a cactus, something, dear lord, anything! But there wasn't a single landmark in sight, just the sand-covered ground stretching all the way to the horizon in every direction.

This has to be a dream, I told myself. I bent down (I almost fell, my legs were shaking so badly) to touch the ground, scooped up a handful of sand, and let it pour out from in between my fingers. It felt courser than the sand I was used to at the beaches of Cape Cod, but it certainly felt real. I pinched my arm, probably harder than I needed to. The pain of the pinch stung, but I didn't wake up. This wasn't a dream.

If I hadn't been freaking out before, I certainly was now, as I realized that the glare and heat from the sun and the details of the ground were far too realistic than any dream that I'd ever had before. My heart somehow found a way to beat even more frantically in my chest and hot tears welled up in my eyes before I suddenly felt dizzy, too. Like, really dizzy. I fell to my knees. The world flashed in and out of view as dark blotches flickered through my line of sight. Suddenly, everything went black.

*****

The next time I woke up, I was still in the desert, and I was again lying on the ground. But when I stood up this time, I saw that I was in a different place than I had been in before. There were a few squat cacti dotting the landscape to my left, and there was a slight incline in the land in front of me. Oh no, no, no, no! How long had I been out?

I looked up at the sun. It seemed to be in the same position it had been the last time I checked. That meant it at least hadn't been hours and hours. I jumped to my feet, shoved the sand off my clothes, and scrambled to start climbing the incline. If only I could see some form of civilization, I could get help. That was what I told myself, over and over again, if only so that my lungs wouldn't explode from stress and fear. Yes, I should focus on finding a town. I could figure out what had happened, or why it had happened. Or maybe, I prayed, this is all just a strangely lucid dream and I'll wake up at any moment. It was the only explanation I could think of that made even the slightest sense.

I stood on the little hill, scanning the horizon. *There!* To my left there was something in the distance, a tiny black blob moving swiftly and smoothly across the sand. A car, it was a car! Which meant that there was a road! Which meant somewhere, I could flag down some form of help. I bolted straight towards the car, but it was a good mile or so away. I sprinted full speed for only about a minute before I found myself doubled over and completely winded. *Come on, Taylor, you can't be that out of shape!*

I passed out.

When I woke up next, I found myself not lying on sand, but on hot asphalt. I jumped to my feet. The road, I was on the road! Behind me there was a tall chain link fence with security cameras on top. That was... unusual. I peered down both sides of the fence, but it seemed to go on and on forever without any gates. *I guess I'm not getting in there,* I thought.

"Hello! Hello! Is anyone here?" I yelled.

There were a few squat, gray buildings several hundred feet away from the fence, and I clung to a desperate hope that my voice was loud enough to travel that far. It must not have been, though, because no one came to my aid. I heard a low rumbling behind me, and to my delight, I turned and saw a car approaching. I waved my arms manically.

"Help! I need help! Please stop the car!" I called.

But the driver didn't even look at me. The man in the camouflaged-patterned jeep just kept on driving, even though I was confident he should have been able to hear my calls.

"Sir! Please!"

I was practically screaming as I chased after the car. But, being in a vehicle cable of much greater speeds than frantic fifteen-year-old girls, the driver zoomed past me, and I, completely winded, fell to my knees again. I tried to fight my dizziness, to see through the patches in my vision. *Stay. Awake!*

"Hey!" A deep voice penetrated my cloudy perception. "HEY!"

I looked up, and saw a pale man in a black suit standing over me. He was another human being, and he was talking to me, so he was everything I had been so desperately looking for, but I was too out of it for my mind to register this. He crouched down beside me and produced a syringe from his pocket. He grabbed my arm. Under normal circumstances, I would have done something to try and stop him, or at least ask what in the world he thought he was doing, but at that point I was too weak and confused to even open my mouth. He looked directly into my eyes, or at least, it seemed like he did. He was wearing sunglasses, and my sight was failing fast.

"Whatever you do," he said, "don't. Move. Everything is going to be fine."

And with that, he jabbed the needle into my skin, and I lost all consciousness.

AREA 51

When I came to this time, the world was strikingly different. I wasn't surrounded by harsh, hot desert anymore, a huge empty sky above me and never-ending yellow-orange sand in every direction. Instead, I lay on a simple, clean white cot, inside a too-cold room with a low black ceiling and an even blacker looking metallic floor and walls. I slowly sat upright, feeling groggier than after I'd awoken from my blackouts before. It was finally dawning on me that this whole situation was just too life-like to be a dream of any kind at all, but whatever it was, I couldn't explain it. Perhaps in the moment that I was pressed against Grandma's grave I had been abducted by aliens. Maybe I had died, and this was what heaven was like. Every possibility I came up with sounded just as ridiculous as the last, and before I knew it there were tears making their way down my face. This all seemed like some sort of confusing, cruel joke. My life had already been falling to pieces, this unexplained adventure was the last thing I needed.

I heard someone moan to the right of me. About ten feet away sat another cot, and about ten feet away from that one was a third. In the cots were two blonde boys that looked like they were about my age. The one closest to me was lying in a way that I couldn't see his face, but his hair was long for a boy, it fell about halfway down his neck in scruffy, golden waves. He was shorter in stature, but he looked fairly muscular, like he lifted weights in his spare time. The farther boy was tall and skinny, with shorter hair and a childlike face, as if he hadn't quite grown up yet. They both seemed unconscious, like I had been just a few moments before.

Click. Click. Click. I whipped my head around to see a black metal door on the wall facing the foot of our cots. Someone was unlocking it and turning the handle. I looked back at the boys to see that the tall one had woken up now, too. Now that he sat upright, I could see that he wore an army-green jacket over a tie-dye T-shirt. We made eye contact, and his expression was one of pure terror, his startlingly blue eyes wide with fear. The door opened.

It the doorway stood the pale man I had seen before, the man who had injected something into my arm just before I had passed out the last time. He looked to me, then at the tall boy. There was a gasp to my right as the other boy sat upright in his cot, swiveling his head around to look at us and struggling for air. His eyes were blue. Like the tall boy's. Like mine.

"I see everyone's awake now," said the pale man. "Come with me. I'll explain as we walk. There's good news and bad news."

He started out the door, but no one followed. I couldn't speak for the other two, but I was paralyzed in shock. Everything was happening so fast.

"Come on now!" insisted the man. "The sooner we get started, the better." He looked right at me and tried to soften his expression. "I won't hurt you, I promise."

Slowly, gingerly, the three of us got off of our cots. The shorter boy took the lead. I fell in line behind everyone else.

"This is a top-secret government research center. Perhaps you've heard of us before," the pale man said. "Welcome to Area 51."

*****

We followed the pale man, who told us his name was Drake, down a long, silver hallway lined with heavy doors on either side. Men in black suits and sunglasses like Drake's passed us but paid us no mind. Drake even walked right through one at one point. Strangely, one of them clipped my shoulder with his brief case, but that passed through my body, too.

"Whoa," whispered the shorter boy.

He he held his right arm straight out beside him as we walked. Not one of the men made any efforts to dodge it; they all walked straight through his arm like ghosts passing through a wall. The boy examined his arm for a moment, then pulled it to his side again, shivering.

Drake finally led us to an open door at the end of the hall. A name and title were stenciled onto the small square window inlayed in the metal: *James D. Mankiw, Special Units Studies and Research.*

Drake pushed open the door, and it moved with a creak, but it also didn't. The door stood perpendicular to its frame, but a pale, ghostly version of it remained sealed shut. Drake walked through the shadow-door as if it were mist and motioned for us to do the same. No one followed. I stared at the strange not-door, too uncertain to move.

"This doesn't make sense now, and I know that," Drake said, "but trust me, children, I can and will explain everything. It won't scare you once you understand it."

I didn't know if I trusted Drake yet, with his too-pale skin, his commanding voice, his precisely-cut and widow's peaked black hair. He reminded me in many ways of a power hungry CEO, an unpredictable hitman, and even a vampire. But his words brought back memories of Grandma, of a five-year-old Taylor crying about the monster in her closet until her Granny picked her up and showed her that the growling she so feared was only the noise of the radiator.

You don't have to cry anymore, honey, she had told me, *you know what it is now. You know it can't hurt you.* I snapped out of my flashback and studied the foggy door. I closed my eyes and stepped through it.

The room inside was small, but crammed full of clutter. A giant computer with three monitors sat on an oversized desk with several sets of drawers below it. Filing cabinets decorated all four corners of the room, and maps of all kinds completely covered the walls. They were dotted with little red thumb tacks that were connected by little red pieces of yarn, like what you see in crime investigation movies.

Drake pushed some papers and books off an overstuffed couch in the middle of the room. He pulled a falling-apart swivel chair from the desk and sat down in it. He gestured to the couch. "Welcome to my office," he said, "please, have a seat."

The Unreal

I sat down, awkward, pressed between two boys I hardly knew. Drake studied us for a moment.

"You probably want to know where you are, and how you got here," he started, slow, deliberate, careful. We nodded. He sighed.

"I never know where to start with these conversations," he said. His eyes flitted from the walls to the floor to the piles and shelves of books, as if looking for something, anything, to distract himself with. "Here," he said, "look around this room. What do you see?"

I examined the objects in the room a little more. There was a lot of *stuff*. Books and papers, mostly.

"A room that needs some cleaning," the short boy mumbled.

"You like maps," said the tall boy.

"Look a little harder," Drake prompted. He picked up some books and handed two to each of us. I examined their titles and covers. *Ghosts of the American Southwest. Mysteries of Ancient Greece. The Advanced Wiccan Spellbook. The Loch Ness Monster: Facts vs. Fiction.* All the books had monsters, ghosts, fairies, skeletons on the covers.

"None of these... these are..." I started.

"They're about things that aren't real," said the short boy, handing his books back to Drake. Drake gave him a wan smile in return.

"Ah," he said, "that's partially correct. To someone living on the organic layer of earth, encountering a vampire or demon wouldn't be something commonly thought as possible. However, we aren't in that layer anymore."

Layers? What was he talking about? Surely he didn't mean the earth's crust, core, and mantle. Before I could respond, Drake continued his speech.

"The layer of Earth that you are used to – that most humans live on and will never leave – is organic because it came from nature. It was created alongside the formation of the Earth, it changes with the evolution of species and the construction of towns and the shifting of earthquakes. It is very much a physical place. On the other end of the spectrum, however, lies an inorganic layer of earth. It exists over the

12

same landmasses, the same islands and mountains and continents, as the first layer does, but it is inhabited by beings created in the minds of humans."

He pulled a notebook off the ground and opened it up.

"Beings like these."

Drake showed a few pages from the notebook. Inside it were sketches of Big Foot, Egyptian gods, Santa Claus.

"Anything that cannot be explicitly proven, but that humans currently do or have at one point believed in, exists within this layer," he said.

I couldn't believe what I was hearing. I mean, it made sense in concept, I guess, but in execution? These things were all myths, stories, fairy tales. Was Drake really trying to tell us that everything we thought was fake existed after all?

"This layer of reality exists on top of and alongside the organic one," Drake continued, "but we cannot see this other layer. So you could be sharing a bedroom with a ghost or monster all your life and never know it."

"So that's where we are? The other layer?" asked the short boy.

Drake smiled again. "Not quite."

His expression changed to one of seriousness. "Beings from the mind layer can travel back and forth between these two layers by passing through the sublayers that lie in between them. Beings gain more power from being believed in. The more a being is believed in, the farther the sublayer it can exist in. If everyone in the world believes in a being, it will cross over into the organic layer forever. The closer the sublayer to the organic layer, the more influence a being will have on the human world. This is why we get Bigfoot and ghost sightings more often than people claim to see the Greek gods. They aren't very believed in anymore," Drake gestured around the room. "And we," he said, "are in one of those sublayers now."

I thought about that for a moment. It would explain why we could pass through the people we saw in the hallways, and why the car I had seen had ignored my calls for help. But I still had so many questions. This still seemed a little sketchy, like it was too weird to be true.

"But... why are we here?" The tall boy asked.

Drake got up, rifled around in a filing cabinet for a moment, then pulled out a thick packet, like the script for a play.

"This is a copy of the Voynich Manuscript," he said. "You might have heard of it before. It's famous for being written in a language that nobody has been able to decipher. No one in your layer knows this, but it was written by a man in the fifteenth century who found out how to travel back and forth between layers, among other magical things. It is essentially a spellbook, written in an almost unbreakable code not even I understand to prevent the information from falling into the wrong hands."

Drake paused for a moment. "Unfortunately, fallen into the wrong hands it has."

He handed the manuscript to me, and I flipped through it. It was covered in strange drawings and words that didn't make any sense, but I guess that was the point.

"Five years ago," Drake said, "there was a man who wanted to enter the other layer of reality to look for two dead relatives. He figured out part of the manuscript and tried to bring himself into the same sublayer as his family, but something went wrong. While he is indeed in a sublayer, he was yet to find who he was looking for. I also believe that he used a sort of combining and replicating spell instead of a locating spell by mistake. He opened a sort of portal to this sublayer, and people are combining into each other and being pulled through it." Drake looked each of us in the eyes. "This is what happened to you. Your bodies and personas were thrown into one area of being, and who you were changed every five minutes. You remained unconscious while you were someone else."

Now *that* was strange. It explained why I kept passing out and waking up in different places, though; the other two boys had been moving me, no, *us,* to different parts of the desert. I looked to the boys on either side of me. Had we really once been connected like that? I shuddered. No, that was creepy to think about.

"People who come through this portal together are usually very similar," Drake continued, "I'm sure you've noticed by now your similarities in appearance and age."

We looked at each other. Blonde hair. Blue eyes. Check.

"Fifteen?" asked the short boy. I shared a glance with the tall boy, and we both nodded.

"In cases like yours a set of three almost always has the same name, too," Drake prompted, looking to the shorter boy.

"Well, I'm Taylor," he said.

"Me too!" the tall boy said. I was stunned; it was my name.

"I am, too," I said quietly. Drake smiled.

"I have something else to explain to you," he said. "Most objects from the layers of earth exist on all planes, but cannot be moved in one layer by someone else moving it in another. In this way, an object exists in all layers, but said object exists independently in each layer."

He looked around the room. "Almost everything here I took from somewhere else," he said. "But this cabinet has been here for ages."

He stood up, grabbed the cabinet, and pulled it away from its corner. It moved, but a faint silhouette remained in the space where it had originally been, almost like a ghost. He tapped the cabinet with his fingers.

"This is where the cabinet is in in our layer," he said, and then pointed to the ghostly vision. "And this is where the cabinet is in the organic, human layer. I can assure you, the same shadow is on the shelves that I took all these books from."

All the information Drake had presented to us before made sense in theory, but this here was physical proof. This was real. I wasn't in the same world anymore.

"However," Drake said, "some objects are special. Cursed, I believe they are often called. I call them universal. They harbor special powers due to their connections to human beliefs, and one of them is shared amongst all layers of reality. I'm sure you've heard of some of them before. The mummy of King Tut. Robert the Doll. Remains from cryptids like the Yeti and the Jersey Devil will often fall into this category as well. The power from these objects can be used to open a portal to a new layer, if one knows the proper way to harness it." He gestured to the Voynich manuscript again as he said this.

"One of the objects the man who entered this sublayer used to make the portal was the corpse of a Chupacabra, a monster from Mexico and Texas. When the spell failed, the dog's face somehow combined with his own. Because of this, if there is an animal nearby when someone is pulled into a sublayer, they will often combine with the animal as well."

He looked to tall Taylor. "Why don't you remove that jacket for us, won't you?" Tall Taylor looked surprised, but he timidly took off the jacket. I gasped.

Two rugged cuts on the back of his shirt revealed two massive red, yellow, and blue feathered parrot wings. He screamed when he saw them, and the wings sprang to life, flapping and fluttering like a chicken who's being chased by a coyote.

"George!" he cried. "George's wings!"

"Don't worry," Drake assured him, "The macaw is fine. His wings still exist on him in the organic layer, but in this layer they exist on you."

That seemed to calm tall Taylor down a bit, but he pulled his jacket back around him hastily, his new wings folding back into place. Drake glanced at the watch on his wrist.

"I think that should answer most of your questions," he said, rising from his chair.

"W-wait," piped up tall Taylor, still frazzled from the realization that he was now part bird. "How come we aren't one person anymore?"

Drake sat back down.

"Electricity," he stated matter-of-factly. "600 volts right as one person changes into the next. I found this out when I was struck by lightning right as I was blacking out five years ago. Unfortunately, my companions fell from a ledge and died. I've been alone here ever since."

He got a faraway look in his eyes for a moment, then continued. "I think it has something to do with the fact that the spell that brought us here was cast using ancient methods in complete darkness. Electricity generates a lot of light and is quite modern. But of course, that's just my theory." He studied each of us for a moment. "You three aren't completely separated, however. I've seen people re-combine before. It happens rarely, but it does happen. But let's not worry about that."

I knew I was going to worry about that. A lot.

"You'll won't be physically able to move more than a mile or so away from each other, and your nerves are still a little jumbled, too."

Before he could react, Drake picked up a heavy hardcover book on fairies and dropped in on short Taylor's toe.

"Ow!" he cried.

But tall Taylor yelped too, and I was terrified to realize that my own foot hurt as well. Drake picked the book back up and struck it across my knee. Judging from their reactions, the boys next to me felt the smack just as much as I had. I looked to each of them in horror. Having to stay within a mile of each other? Being able to feel their pain? What kind of problems would that cause?

With that another though crossed my mind. *Wait a minute, just how long was I going to be here?* The way Drake was talking, it seemed as if he was trying to prepare us, trying to teach us the ins and outs of this new world only because we were going to have to navigate it ourselves soon enough.

"How do we get out of here?" I asked. I looked to Drake in a panic. "*Can* we get out of here?"

An expression of pity crossed his face.

"That's why I've brought you here," he said, "I'm going to need your help with that."

*****

We followed Drake into a larger room. The walls here were a lighter gray instead of black, the ceiling was higher, and the walls were covered in weapons, tents, backpacks, and other supplies.

"I told you all earlier about how some artifacts can be used to open doors to new layers," he said, and we all nodded. "I've been trying to secure enough of these objects to send us all back to the organic layer. However, at the same time, the man who brought us here has been collecting these objects so he can send us into the layer of human belief. This has made both finding them, and keeping them, more difficult than it would normally be," he said.

"That's where people like you come in. I believe there are about 200 sets of people wandering around this layer of reality. I've rescued 23, and sent 21 of them on missions to retrieve special objects for me. 10 are still out there on missions now. The others..." his voice trailed off for a moment. "They didn't quite make it."

He paused and took off his sunglasses. His eyes were such a dark shade of brown that I couldn't tell his pupil from his iris.

"Listen," he said, his voice soft now, "I'm going to be honest with you. It's dangerous out there. There are thousands of beings that inhabit this layer of reality, and many of them can kill you. I won't make you do anything you don't want to do. I can get you some rooms, and you can wait things out here, where it's safe, until I find a way back. But I could really use you. You could go home much sooner if you went searching than if you waited here. For all I know, you could end up waiting forever."

Both options terrified me. On one hand, I could run around a strange new world with two people I barely knew, trying not to die by the hands of horrible monsters I'd barely be able to protect myself from, looking for objects I'd barely heard of. Or, I could end up living forever in a universe where a normal life wasn't possible.

My grandma, before she had retired, had been a nurse. She used to tell me stories of her time working in the ER and on World War II battlefields, stories of not only saving lives, but of improving them. I wanted to follow in her footsteps, to do what she had done, to honor her legacy and make her proud. And now that she was gone, the last part seemed more important than ever. I couldn't get a career in this place. I couldn't live the life I wanted.

Drake cleared his throat. "If you three need some time to talk about this, I can step outsi—"

"I'll go!" I said, louder than I meant to. I looked to the other Taylors standing beside me. "I'll go if you guys will."

A moment of silence. Then, "I think we should go, too," said short Taylor, puffing his chest and stepping forward. I held my breath and turned towards tall Taylor. He looked back at me, then smiled.

"I guess we're going on an adventure, then," he said. An expression of relief and pride slid across Drake's face.

"Alright then," he said. "Let's find an adventure for you."

Drake opened his notebook and flipped through the pages. "I have something special I want you to find," he said. "It's at the Warren's Occult Museum in Connecticut. Getting there will be the easy part. I've drive you to the airport, where you can hop on a human plane, then get into someone's car once the plane lands. Get as close as you can, then start walking."

He showed us a picture taped to one of the pages. It was of a Raggedy Ann doll, sitting inside a wooden box with a glass front, hanging on a wall.

"This is the Annabelle doll," Drake said, "it is said to be haunted by a demon, and it has supposedly led to the death of at least one man. You might have to pick the lock on the case, and there may be a spirit from another layer clinging to it that you'll have to wrestle it from, but this should be a relatively easy first quest."

Alright, that doll's picture looked harmless enough. This couldn't be too hard.

"Once you secure the doll," he continued, "you'll need to get it back to me before I can send you after a second object."

He produced an apple and spray bottled filled with a bright pink liquid from his pocket. He sprayed the liquid on the fruit.

"SCREEEEEEEEEE!!!"

I froze as an ungodly screech echoed from the corridor in front of us, and a dark shape came flying out of it at a million miles per hour. Before anyone could react, the shape had swooped down, grabbed the fruit from Drake, and perched on top of the gun rack. It sat in a crouch, cradling the apple in its hands and nibbling on its new treasure.

It appeared to be a monster of some sort. Its body looked muscular, like that of a human bodybuilder, but it was covered in a light brown hair, like the fur on a horse's body. It had long claws on its hands and feet, and giant, paper-thin butterfly-shaped wings on its back. Its head was the strangest part. It was that of an insect, complete with huge red eyes and antennae. Drake reached up and patted the creature's leg. It let out a gentle purring noise but didn't look up from its snack. It seemed friendly enough, but I couldn't help feeling a little skittish around such a large, strange creature.

"This," Drake said, "is Mothman."

The word was an accurate description, to say the least.

"He terrorized the town of Point Pleasant, West Virginia, during the 1960s," Drake said, "his notoriety has decreased a bit, but he still gets some attention from TV specials and his museum every now and then. He lives in this sublayer, and he's been helping me out quite a bit."

Mothman finished off his apple and looked at Drake hungrily. "Screeee?" he croaked. Drake patted his knee and held out the bottle to tall Taylor.

"Mothman here can't see very well, but his sense of smell is impeccable. Once you find the doll, spray this on some fruit or meat, and he'll come to you within a few hours." He plucked a simple flip phone off the wall and placed it in short Taylor's hand. "Once you've given him the doll, send me a text so I know when to summon him back."

"Ruuuuuurrrrr," purred Mothman as he climbed down from the gun rack to stand beside Drake. He eyed us with a curious caution and cocked his head to the side. Drake pulled three black backpacks off the wall. "Come on," he said, "I'll help you start packing."

ANNABELLE

Two hours later we got out of Drake's car at the Las Vegas airport, me and the other Taylors each carrying a backpack filled with food, spare clothing, and other supplies.

"Well," Drake said, "this is as far as I can take you. You know how to contact me if you need anything." Short Taylor patted his right jacket pocket, just to make sure the cell phone was still there. It was.

"Scraaaaaaawww!!" cried Mothman, eyeing the giant light fixtures hanging from the metal overhang of the entrance. He fluttered up to one, flying into and around it repeatedly.

Drake sighed. "I'm sorry, I don't know why I let him come along," he said. He turned to look at each of us, with sadness in his eyes. "Be careful out there, please," he said, "I've lost so many good people already." He shook each of our hands. "The best of luck to each of you." He removed another apple from his pocket and threw it at Mothman.

"EEEEEE!!!!" Mothman cried.

"To the car! Come on!" Drake replied.

Mothman sank to the ground dejectedly and climbed into the passenger seat. Drake took the wheel and started the engine. And then they were gone.

And there I was, alone at a strange airport with two strange boys I was somehow supposed to be so connected to, yet barely knew. We stood in silence for a moment, no one quite sure what to do. Finally, short Taylor spoke.

"Well," he said, "I guess we should find the next flight to Hartford." He pulled open one of the huge front doors and walked inside. I followed him.

*****

"We should probably think of something to call ourselves," tall Taylor said as we searched for a flight schedule. "We can't all be Taylor."

Short Taylor looked over his shoulder at him. He had been leading us around this whole time. He claimed he hadn't been to this airport before, but he sure acted like he had.

"Fine," he said, "I can be Tay, then."

Tall Taylor turned to me. My mind was blank. I could have gone by my middle name, Mildred, but it's kind of awful sounding and I was too shy to suggest that tall Taylor go by his middle name instead. He studied me for a moment, the gears of his mind turning. "You could be Lori," he finally said, "you know, from Tay-LOR."

Lori. I hated it. That was a name for girls who were cheerleaders and who went to parties and talked to everyone and talked too loud and didn't read books or like museums. That wasn't the type of girl I was. But I didn't have any other ideas, and I thought telling tall Taylor I hated his suggestion would be rude.

"Okay," I mumbled.

Tay glanced back at us. "Then you'll just be Taylor," he said to tall Taylor, cutting off any chance of him getting a "fun" nickname as well.

The airport was crowded with people. Families on vacation, official-looking men and women on business trips, and twenty-somethings arriving in town to party. But none of them could see us, and it was a strange concept to get used to. I tried to apologize for bumping into people several times before I remembered I couldn't bump into people at all. When we found a flight schedule and stopped to look at it, a few people walked right through us. It was creepy; I felt like I was a ghost.

Tay traced down the board with his finger.

"There!" he exclaimed, tapping a line that read Hartford, Flight 264, 6:30, Gate 24. "That leaves in twenty minutes." That wasn't much time to find Gate 24, but at least that didn't mean we had hours and hours to wait. "I'm pretty sure it's this way," Tay said, walking to the left.

It turned out that the gate was to the right, not to the left, but we still made it there just as people were starting to board. It was odd, skipping the line and just walking onto an airplane with no ticket. But no one noticed us, of course, and we slid into a row near the back of the plane, with Tay taking the window seat, Taylor by the aisle, and me in the middle. Unfortunately, another set of three people decided they would be sitting in our row as well. They went right through us, but it was still extremely eerie and just plain awkward to have another person sitting inside of you. We got up, but it was a full flight, so we sat down in a small strip of empty space between the bathroom and the back row.

Tay groaned, rested his head against the wall, and closed his eyes. Taylor sat with his legs straight in front of him, watching the other passengers with an expression of genuine curiosity. I sat hugging my knees, feeling awkward and unsure of myself. I had always been so shy; I almost would have preferred finding the doll alone. I mean, sure, I wanted to talk to my companions, to befriend the people I would be navigating this complex world with, but I just didn't know how. What did we have in common besides situation and appearance? Surely their grandmas hadn't just died as well.

"Where are you guys from?" Taylor asked, breaking the silence. I felt really timid at that moment, so I waited for Tay to answer first. There was another beat of silence.

"San Francisco," Tay said finally, without opening his eyes.

"Concord," I whispered.

I wanted to know where Taylor was from, too, but I was too afraid to ask, and Tay obviously didn't care. So we just sat there quietly.

"I'm from St. Louis," he offered. No one reacted.

He stood up and walked down the aisle of the plane, leaving me alone with Tay. I turned my head and got a really good look at him for the first time. His eyes where still closed, his head resting against the wall. He seemed so careless, like everything that had just happened in the last 5 hours or so was completely routine. How could he be so relaxed? I took a closer look at his face. He reminded me a little of an illustration of the Greek god Apollo in a book I had owned as a child: longish golden hair, flawless tanned skin, clean-shaven and chiseled features. He was dressed more like a hipster than a god, though, with ripped up jeans and a white T-shirt under a blue and black flannel. He opened his eyes and caught me staring, and I quickly turned away, hiding my face with my hair.

I was glad to see that Taylor had returned right then. In his arms were a pen and one of those napkins the stewardesses hand you with the drinks they serve.

"Okay," he said, drawing a crude outline of the United States on the napkin and placing it on the carpet so that the three of us could all look at it together. "So, we started here," he drew a star in the lower right hand corner of the map, representing his best guess as to where Las Vegas was. "And it's about a seven-hour flight to here." Another star for Hartford. "But the doll isn't in Hartford, is it?" he asked.

"No, it's in Monroe," I said, remembering what Drake had told us. "It's a little bit west of there."

"So how do we get there?" Tay said, sitting up now. "We could hitch-hike, but we'd have to find somebody going that way first. That might be hard if we can't talk to anyone."

"There might be a bus going there, too," Taylor said, "we could look for one when we land."

"Yeah, but we can't depend on something that might not even exist," Tay responded.

I thought about it for a moment. How could we figure out where everyone was going? I looked around the plane. A lot of the passengers would probably be staying in the city, but surely some of them lived in the suburbs and were coming back from vacations. There aren't that many airports in Connecticut, after all. We just needed a way to figure out where people lived. But an address is something that you don't always say aloud too often, especially when you're driving yourself or your family home, because you know where you're going.

"We could check everyone's ID," I said, "that'll tell us where they live, at least."

The two boys paused for a moment, pondering my idea.

"That... would work," Tay said.

We decided to start by searching any purses we could find, since it was less awkward than digging around in people's pants pockets. I grabbed a handbag from a sleeping woman in the front row. Her name was Julie Stanton, and she lived in Middletown. Not what I was looking for. Emily Steele, from New Britain. No. Marissa Crawley, from Essex. Way too far South. Erica Bartley lived in Oxford. That wasn't too far from Monroe, we could hitch a ride with her and then walk—

"I found someone!" Tay called, "Meredith Dabrowski. 2274 Silverton Drive, Monroe, Connecticut." Taylor and I rushed over to him in excitement, and he proudly showed us the driver's license. He pointed to the woman it belonged to — a brown-haired lady dressed in business attire, silently reading a novel in her seat. "When the plane lands, whatever you do," he said, "don't lose sight of that woman!"

After five hours of trying to sleep, trying to find something to do, and just plain sitting on the ground worrying, the plane landed in Hartford. We ran down the aisle to stand next to our guide. We followed her off the plane to the baggage claim, where she took a large blue suitcase off the conveyor and out to her car, a simple white station wagon. We packed ourselves like sardines into the tiny, lumpy seats in the back. Meredith fired up the engine, and then we were off.

I looked out the window as we drove. It was dark now, around midnight, and all the street lights and neon storefront signs shown obnoxiously though the otherwise peaceful darkness. We weren't that far from Concord, my home, and we were even closer to Providence, my soon-to-be home. A startling realization passed my mind.

Oh my gosh, no one knows where I am! My cousin was supposed to pick me up at 10 o'clock tomorrow, what would she think when she came to get me and I wasn't there? What would my friends think when I didn't answer their texts or emails for days? Would I be reported missing? The thought made me sick to my stomach; I didn't want to worry anyone; they might think I'd run away or been killed. And no matter how hard they'd search they'd never be able to find me.

My anxious stupor was cut short when I heard a gasp from Taylor. I looked outside his window and gasped too. Running through the woods beside the highway was a giant black dog, at least ten feet long and six feet tall, with massive, bulging muscles in its front legs. It was running almost as fast as the car was. It raced parallel to the car for a few more seconds, and then veered off to the right, into the woods and away from the vehicle. Taylor and I looked at each other, wide-eyed. A bad taste filled my mouth. This must have been one of the monsters that lived within our sublayer. If they all were as frightening as that, though, I didn't really want to find out what else lived in those woods.

It only took about half an hour before we reached Meredith's apartment. We wrestled our bags out of her car and studied the map of Monroe that Drake had given us.

"Okay," Tay said, "it's only about a fifteen-minute walk from here. We could probably steal this doll in less than an hour."

I hoped he was right. I thought about what Drake had told us – that there could be spirits in our own sublayer clinging to the doll. It wasn't a pleasant thought, but what choice did we have? We had already come all this way, it would be foolish not to at least try to take the doll. On that note, we started walking.

I knew we were at the right address, but it certainly didn't look like a museum. It looked like your average middle-class country home, complete with a cutesy red-brick chimney and an American flag hanging from the porch. The only thing that set this house apart from its neighbors was a carved wooden sign hung near one of the windows: *New England Paranormalology Research Center.*

"I... guess this is it," Tay said. Taylor and I followed him up the front porch and helped him pick the lock with a bobby pin and a hammer from his bag. We got the door open, but a ghostly yellow shadow stood in its place. It was still safely closed in the real world; no one would ever know we were here. We took our flashlights out of our backpacks and stepped inside.

The first floor was a living room, not a gallery. A couch with a white quilt draped over its back sat on a yellow-patterned rug, and ceramic knick-knacks decorated wooden bookshelves. There appeared to be a kitchen or dining room to the left. The air smelled faintly of fresh-baked cookies and old wood.

"Where the heck is the museum?" Tay whispered. I shrugged. Surely this wasn't it. Unless, those clay roosters were really possessed by demons, and those books were all titles about Satanism, and there was a pentagram hiding under that rug, and—

"Maybe she keeps the doll up here?" he suggested, looking to me for an answer. That didn't explain why this house was considered a museum, but I didn't have another solution. A Raggedy Ann doll actually would've fit in with the calm country-homestead theme of the room.

Tay nodded. "Maybe, let's start—"

"Guys!" Taylor called. He stood in front of an open door that led to a set of descending stairs. "I think I found the museum." It was in the basement, of course! This must have been the Warren's house, and they kept their displays separate from their living room.

I tiptoed over to where Taylor was standing and shined my flashlight down the staircase. Newspaper clippings and creepy paintings lined the walls. If that wasn't the museum entrance, nowhere was.

At the bottom of the stairwell was a simple wooden hallway with a few lightbulbs hanging from the ceiling. It could have been your average unfinished basement; except for what hung on the walls. There were more framed newspaper clippings about Ed and Lorraine Warren: they had been Demonologists in their heyday, apparently, and had spent a lot of time creeping around New England's most haunted houses. There were paintings on the wall, too, all credited to Ed Warren. One was of a big black dog standing in a pinewood forest, not unlike the one I had seen running beside Meredith's car. Another painting was of an evil-looking house, and another of a weeping ghostly figure. I shined my light on the opposite wall and jumped back, startled to see a mold of a pale, screaming head coming out of a picture frame.

It's not real, I told myself, *It's just decoration. Like for Halloween.*

The hallway ended, and we turned into the main section of the museum, a large room even darker than the hallway.

"I-I think that's a light switch," Taylor whispered. He turned it on, and a faint bronze light filled the room, and a soundtrack of a creepy children's church choir began to play. In the very back of the room, a bright light inside a wooden case flickered to life, showcasing the Annabelle doll that sat inside of it.

Even with the lights on, the room was still fairly dark, which made the contents inside of it a thousand times creepier. It wasn't the kind of museum I was used to, with objects carefully sorted into display cases with neat little information cards explaining each and every one. Instead, the room resembled more of a garage sale or a messy second hand store – stuff crammed onto every nook and cranny, including on the walls and floor, with no discernible order or pattern. Nothing was accompanied by a display card, and nothing was behind glass.

The problem was, these artifacts were exactly the kind you'd want tucked away into a locked case, more for your safety than for theirs. A mannequin dressed in a bridal gown with a slash mark across her throat. An Ouija board with a glowing red lightbulb and bronze dagger lying across it. A stuffed tiger skin rug with the mouth frozen in a fang-filled scream. Human skulls, satanic figurines, and terrifying dolls galore, dolls that almost made Annabelle look innocent and safe. There was a three-foot-tall figure with black feathers for hair and a contorted scream on its paper white face, a simple rag doll that hung from a noose, and seven-foot-tall papier mache humanoid sculpture with horns on its head. It reminded me off the monster with eyes in its hands from that horror movie I had to watch for Spanish class, Pan's Labyrinth, and the comparison made me shudder. That movie had given me nightmares for a week.

Trying our best not to bump into or step on anything, we slowly made our way to the Annabelle doll. I followed Tay and Taylor, scared enough that there was no way I was going first. Tay led the way instead, but I could see the fear on his face, too. We stood in front of the doll's glass and wood box. She seemed to be the only thing deemed dangerous enough to warrant a protective case.

Warning, read a white sign on the bottom of the glass window, *positively do not open.* I wished we could have obeyed that warning. Taylor turned away from the case, shivering.

"We aren't alone here," he said, his voice trembling. He was right. We hadn't seen any beings from our sublayer yet, but there was no way there weren't any in a place as unholy as this. If they weren't in our layer, they were hiding within a different one. I could feel them, could feel them watching us.

"C-come on, man!" Tay said. "Let's just grab the doll and go." Taylor took a deep, shaky breath, then shut his eyes and opened the case. I wasn't quite sure what compelled me to, but it was me who reached up and took the doll. I shut my eyes tight and held my breath, waiting for the fallout.

But nothing happened. No demon attacked us, no ghost cursed us, the doll did not erupt into flames. I cradled Annabelle in my arms. She was soft, just like a stuffed animal would be, and her face was calm and gentle, soothing, even. I looked up a Tay and Taylor.

"So... that's it? Can we leave?" Tay asked. I glanced back down at the doll, then up at him. I couldn't believe our luck. We had the doll, didn't we?

"Yeah... I guess so." *That wasn't so bad,* I thought to myself as we walked towards the door. Unfortunately, the thought was premature. Barely a moment after, everything went bad.

A snow-white glowing ball of light shot out of the doll and disappeared into the chaos of the museum. We stopped dead in our tracks and looked at each other in horror. Tay's eyes were wider than golf balls. "What was—"

An unholy screech echoed from a table nearby. The feather haired doll's head had turned 180 degrees to face us. Before we could react, it jumped off the table and charged straight for us. Tay screamed at the top of his lungs and kicked the doll so hard it flew across the room, hitting the wall with a hard *thump!* and slumping to the floor. The same light that had shot out of Annabelle flew out of the defeated doll and flew into the seven-foot-tall man. The monster blinked for a moment, then turned his head to the right. It started towards us, walking slowly with its arms outstretched, as if asking for one final hug before it snapped our necks.

"Hell no!" Tay cried, throwing his flashlight at the monster as hard as he was able before ducking behind Taylor. It hit the creature square in the chest, sending it tumbling backward. The light left its body and flew into the tiger skin. The tiger's stuffed head roared, and Taylor bolted for the exit. Tay and I scrambled after him, only to see the ball of light zoom right over our heads and down the hall.

"Oh no, oh *heck* no!" Tay yelled. "We're finding another way out. I'm not going in there with that thing."

"There's no time!" I cried, and by cried, I mean I really was very close to crying. "Please, the longer we stay here the more time it has to kill us!"

I pushed past him and ran down the hall, hopeful that if I just could move fast enough I could outrun whatever trick the orb had waiting for us. I could hear Tay and Taylor's hurried footsteps close behind me, and a scream from a painting above me. I buried my face in Annabelle's, not wanting to see anymore nightmare fuel. I trotted up the stairs, my face already soaking with sweat.

Wait... how could that be? The water on my face felt hotter than sweat, thicker than sweat...

I looked down at Annabelle, only to see that the doll had become drenched in dark red blood, blood that had stained my face and shirt, blood that spread around her mouth in just the right way to paint an evil grin on her face. I screamed a scream louder than I had ever imagined I could, filled with pure terror as I full-on sprinted out the front door. The ball of light left the doll's body and the bleeding stopped, but I kept bolting as far away as I could. I had made it all the way across the street when I heard Tay's voice calling me: "Lori! It's gone! Stop running!"

I stopped running. Tay and Taylor were keeled over in the street, panting and gasping for air. I walked over to them and wordlessly placed the doll in Tay's arms. I took the backpack off Taylor's shoulders, pulled out and apple and a pink spray bottle, and summoned Mothman.

MERCY

We started walking away from the museum almost immediately, frazzled, unsettled, and eager to find a hotel. Despite the bleeding incident earlier, I still clung to Annabelle like my life depended on it. After all we had been through to get her, there was no way I was letting her out of my sight.

"Okay," Tay said, turning and walking backwards so he could look at Taylor and I. "I can feel someone's heel bleeding, and it's not mine."

It had been so long since our talk with Drake, I had almost forgotten we could feel each other's pain. I examined the backs of my feet, and sure enough, a great gash sat bleeding at the top of my heel. I hadn't even noticed it.

"Sorry," I mumbled. Tay let out an exasperated sigh and ran his fingers through his hair. "O-kay!" he said. "Anybody know first aid?"

"I do," I said. I set down my backpack and dug through it for the first aid kit Drake had given us.

"SCREEEEEEEEEE!" a gust of air rushed towards me as Mothman landed beside me and snatched the apple from Taylor's hand. He flew up to a nearby pine tree branch to devour the fruit. I cleaned and bandaged my heel while we waited, with Annabelle sitting on my lap. Tay pulled out the phone to tell Drake that Mothman had arrived. Taylor sat down next to me, cross-legged, watching the stars.

Our mothy friend finished his treat and descended from the tree, watching us expectantly. I rose from my spot on the ground and gingerly handed Annabelle to Mothman. He looked from me to the doll. "Screeee?"

"Take that back to Drake," I told him, "be very careful. Don't lose her." He suddenly turned his head to the left, nostrils and antennae flaring.

"SCREEEEeeeeeEEEEEeeeeeEEEE!!" he cried as he rocketed away from us at the speed of light, having smelled Drake's own bottle of pink spray at Area 51. Almost as soon as Mothman left, the phone in Tay's pocket buzzed.

"It's Drake," he said. He flipped the phone open and held it to his ear. "Hello?"

We talked to Drake on speaker phone as we continued to look for a hotel along the highway. We told him everything that had happened, from the Warren's normal living room to the creepy music in the basement to the orb of light bringing the artifacts to life to the doll bleeding in my arms. He was silent for a moment when we finished, thinking hard.

"That ball of light you saw sounds like a poltergeist of sorts," he said, "it's a very powerful type of spirit that has the ability to move objects around a sublayer or the human layer, depending on where it resides. Before the Warrens acquired it, the Annabelle doll was said to have walked around the apartment it was kept in while the owners weren't home. It bled just like you described, too, but the Warrens always suspected what possessed it was demonic in nature. Honestly, with all the unholy artifacts stored in that museum, I'm surprised you didn't have something worse happen to you."

"Then why the hell would you send us there on a first mission!? You knew that place was going to be a whole other level of dangerous!" Tay yelled into the phone. Taylor and I froze, nervous for Drake's retaliation.

Taylor cleared his throat. "Um, Tay—"

"Shut it!" Tay whipped his head backwards and gave Taylor a death stare.

A long sigh came from Drake's end of the line. "I'm afraid that was one of the least dangerous missions I could have given you," he said. No one answered him for a moment. Wait, *what*? Living, bleeding dolls and screaming tiger skins were the *least* danger we could be in?

"What do you mean?" Tay asked.

"All the artifacts I need from you have something dark about them," Drake said, "most of them will have something guarding them, that's just the way these universal objects work. Items that aren't powerful wouldn't exist within all layers, you know."

I knew Drake had a point, but what he said put a sour taste in my mouth.

"I have another mission lined up for you," he continued, "but it will most likely be even more frightening than the last. All your other missions will be, too. If you would like to come back to Area 51, you are more than welcome to catch another flight."

No, we couldn't go back, I knew that now. Stealing the doll had been more than terrifying in the moment, but we had made it out okay, hadn't we? Besides, I wasn't about to sit back and just wait for the day when everything got better, when we finally got to leave the sublayer of the Unreal. I had to *make* it better, to do the dirty work myself.

"We can't stop now," I said to Tay and Taylor. They looked at me, Taylor biting his lip with fear and worry, Tay holding tears behind his eyes. I wasn't sure what else to say to them. What in the world could I do to comfort them, to assure them that we'd be fine, that we wouldn't die in this strange, crazy world? I didn't know, but I wasn't going back to Drake without a fight.

"We... we can't wait for this to fix itself. I need to go home," I said. I glanced down at the doll's blood that stained my shirt. "We've done this much already."

"She's right," said Drake over the phone. "You have done very well for yourselves. You've secured a very powerful object without any help in less than 24 hours."

Tay bit his lip, and squeezed his eyes shut tight. "What... what would our next mission be?" he asked.

"In Exeter, Rhode Island, there is the grave of a girl named Mercy Brown. She was purported to be a vampire by all the townspeople, including her own father. I need you to dig up her grave and steal her skull," Drake said matter-of-factly.

Grave robbing?! Pulling the head off a corpse?! The thought of it made me want to vomit, but I *needed* to go home.

"Oh, god," muttered Tay. Taylor's face turned paper white.

"Now, now, it won't be as bad as you're thinking," Drake added quickly, "there is little doubt that this girl was not really a vampire in life; her family needed a scapegoat as for why her brother was sick with tuberculosis. They dug up her body to find that it had not decayed even though she had been dead for weeks, and they mutilated the corpse to calm their fears and cure her brother. That was well over a hundred years ago, however, and I can assure you that while the soil may have been too cold for her to properly decompose during her first few weeks in the ground, she is little more than a pile of bones now."

Tay didn't respond, his eyes wide with terror.

I have to get home, I kept repeating to myself, *I have to get home for Grandma.* I walked over, plucked the phone from his hand, and said, "We'll do it."

We found a hotel after twenty more exhausting minutes of walking, then followed a man who was just checking in to his room. We pulled the blankets and pillows off his bed and took a few more from the closet; sleeping in the bed with a strange man would have felt weird and uncomfortable, and there wasn't room for all of us anyway. We each arranged our own little makeshift sleeping bag on the floor. Tay and Taylor elected to let me take the first shower, given that my face, shirt, and hair were still coated in doll blood.

I dug a spare t-shirt and jeans out of my backpack and shut the bathroom door behind me. The hot water felt nice, but seeing the blood run off my body and collect on the tub floor was eerie and sickening, and looked like something straight out of a horror movie. The sight of blood normally didn't faze me much, given how much time I spent volunteering at the hospital, but it made me squeamish to see so much of the crimson fluid on my own body. The sight made me feel like I was dying.

I dried myself off and put on the fresh clothing. The shirt was a few sizes too big, but I could make do. *I CLIMBED THE GREAT WALL OF CHINA!* the light green shirt proclaimed, with a black outline of a section of the Great Wall below the expression. I, however, had not climbed the Great Wall, and briefly wondered where Drake had found a shirt like this. *Maybe he's been to China*, I thought, before deciding he'd probably just taken it from a thrift store.

I climbed under the blankets on my section of the floor and Tay went into the bathroom next. The real-layer man laid in bed reading a book, and Taylor was doodling with the hotel provided pen and notepad. I wanted to ask what he was drawing, but again, my shyness held me back. Why had talking to him and Tay been so much easier back at the museum? *Because there wasn't time to think,* I told myself, there had been no time to worry about whether what I said was stupid or not or if anyone cared for my opinion or would get mad at me for saying the wrong thing. *Come on, you've been through so much with him already, he probably wants to talk to you, too.*

"W-what are you drawing?" I finally spat out my question.

Taylor looked up from his artwork, startled. He glanced back down at it again. It was all just a bunch of incoherent lines and shapes to me. I guess he was seeing the same thing I was, though, because he said, "I don't really know." He picked the pen back up and went right on doodling. Um, okay.

I heard the shower turn off in the bathroom. The man in the bed yawned and flipped off the light switch. I was feeling awkward, uncomfortable, lonely, and scared, and I needed a hug from my grandma now more than ever, but I put my head on my pillow and fell asleep. There was nothing else I could do.

I woke up the next morning to a bright light shining in my face. I slowly opened my eyes and saw Taylor tugging open the curtains, letting a thick wave of sunlight into the room. Tay groaned and turned over.

"It's ten o'clock. We should probably get going," Taylor said. I sat up and looked at the clock on the bedside table. 10:02. Yes, it was probably time to start walking.

We grabbed some bagels and fruit from the hotel lobby and sat down at a table with a map of New England I'd taken from the brochure rack. The distance from here to Exeter was too far to walk, but it would be less than a two-hour drive. We decided our best bet was to walk to the highway that went to Rhode Island and hop in a car.

We hitchhiked our way down the highway, getting out of cars when they paused at the first stoplight off the exit ramp and getting back into ones that merged back onto the highway. It took a few hours more than it should have, but we eventually made it to Exeter. We left our last car on just the outskirts of the city, so we wandered our way downtown, trying to find Chestnut Hill Baptist Church Cemetery.

"Wait!" Taylor cried as we passed a hardware store, "If we're going to be digging up a grave, we're probably going to need a shovel. I'll be right back." He dashed inside the store, leaving me standing on the sidewalk with Tay. We waited in silence for a few moments, watching Taylor search for a shovel through the storefront window.

Tay nudged me in the ribs with his elbow. "Hey," he said, "you did a good job back there. With Annabelle, I mean. If I was holding that doll when it started bleeding, I don't think I would've been able to keep my cool."

I smiled. "Thanks," I said. Another moment of silence passed before I worked up the courage to say, "You did a good job too, though, killing the first two monsters."

Tay laughed. "Oh god, that was just instinct. That demon doll creeped me out from the moment I saw it, and then when it just came running straight at me, and I was just thinking, *oh no you don't! Nope! I'm out!*"

We both laughed this time. "Dang, how do those people live with all that stuff in their basement? I don't think I'd ever get any sleep in that place," he said.

Taylor emerged from the store then, holding three long metal shovels. He handed one to each of us, and we wordlessly continued our search for the cemetery.

Taylor had cut two holes in his new shirt for his wings, and was trying to use them as we walked. He could hover a few inches off the ground for a second or two, but he couldn't get much farther than that, especially not while carrying a heavy shovel in one hand. Tay extended his hand to him.

"Here, I'll hold that," he said, "I want to see what those babies can do."

Taylor handed off the shovel and took a deep breath. He sprinted forward for about twenty feet, then jumped. He hovered about a foot off the ground for a moment, his wings flapping and fluttering chaotically as they tried desperately to keep him in the air, before he tumbled downward and slid a few feet in a rough landing. Tay covered his mouth with his hand, choking back laughter. I glared at him and rushed over to Taylor. I gave him my hand and helped him up.

"Are you okay?" I asked. He brushed the dirt off his shirt and pants, nodding. Tay stood beside us now, his expression sobered.

"Hey, you'll get better at it, man," he said, "everything takes time."

We ate dinner by taking food off the tables of a pizza place, each of us wolfing down a slice as we walked. It was Tay's idea, saying that he wanted to find the cemetery and leave as soon as possible. It was smart thinking, because we arrived at the cemetery just as the sun was starting to set. It was small, so it didn't take long to find Mercy's grave:

MERCY L.
daughter of
George T. & Mary E.
BROWN
Died Jan. 17, 1892,
Aged 19 years.

I hadn't realized she had died so young. It felt wrong, but we started digging.

It turns out that digging a six-foot hole in the ground takes a very long time and is quite tiring. We passed the time by playing word games like twenty questions. Taylor's turn always took the longest because he would think of the oddest and most specific things: a dragon scale, the label on a soup can, the sign of a coffee shop we had passed a few hours ago. We had to take a lot of breaks from digging, during which we'd switch to playing I Spy instead. Again, Taylor would choose very specific things to spy: the letter A on my shirt, one particular leaf on a tree, Tay's left pinky finger. A part of me thought it would be nice to be as creative as he was. The other part of me was frustrated at how much harder it was to finish each round he played.

It was dark by the time our shovels hit a piece of soft wood. We scraped away the last bits of dirt to reveal a simple oak coffin. It was decided, through an intense rock-paper-scissors tournament, that Taylor would be the one to open the coffin and pry the skull from Mercy's body. He would then hand the skull to me while Tay helped him out of the six-foot-deep hole.

Tay hoisted himself out of the grave, then pulled me up after him. We lied down on the grass and peered over the edge of the pit, watching Taylor in case something went wrong. And judging by what had happened with our last mission, we were very concerned that something was going to go wrong.

Taylor took a deep breath. "Alright, on the count of three," Tay said, his voice shaking. He looked at me and nodded. We counted together.

"One, Two..."

Taylor tore the lid off the coffin. Inside lay a skeleton in a once-beautiful, ragged purple dress with a gash down the chest.

Mercy.

A foul stench filled the air, but not quite as foul as I had expected. She really had been dead for a long time, and I was grateful for that.

Taylor shut his eyes tight and put his hands around Mercy's skull, a repulsed look crossing his face. He pulled it away from her body with a sickening *snap!* He exhaled shakily and handed me the head. I took it, careful not to drop the mandible, and cringed; it was repulsive to be holding a part of a dead person.

Tay was struggling to get Taylor out of the grave. Taylor flapped his wings in a useless attempt to help. He had managed to get himself a few inches off the ground when a skeletal hand grabbed his ankle. He screamed bloody murder, which caused Tay to panic and drop his wrists, which caused Taylor to plummet downwards onto Mercy's corpse, landing on her bones with an awful crunch.

"*NOOOOOOOO!!!*"

An anguished screech emanated from the ground. Taylor's wings suddenly worked just fine as he shot up from the grave at top speed. A collection of white mist and a piece of broken wood from the coffin rose up from the grave after him. It hovered above the tombstone and condensed into the ghostly figure of a girl with long, light brown hair and a purple gown. But this was no friendly ghost. She had pale, scarred, rotting skin. The entirety of each of her eyes was no color but jet black. Blood stained the front of her dress and dripped from the corners of her mouth.

She whirled the wood at Taylor before I could even comprehend what I was seeing, but he dove out of the way, crashing chin-first into a low-laying gravestone. Pain seared across my jaw and a scream of terror ripped out of my throat. The ghost spun around to me, fire blazing in her dark eyes, her glare like death. She saw the skull in my hands.

"YOU!" she cried as she charged at me, swooping downward with the speed of an undead fighter jet. I screamed again and fell backward to dodge the rabid ghost, worried that I'd crack the cranium if I wasn't careful.

"Leave her alone!" cried Tay as he threw a stone at the angry spirit. It went right through her, of course, with her being a ghost and all, but it was enough of a distraction that she turned her fury on him.

He spread his arms in a *come at me, bro!* type gesture, then picked up a second rock. The ghost screamed and rushed towards him, and his brave facade evaporated as he dodged behind a tree.

Taylor was up now. A beard of blood had formed from a gash on his chin. He carried the lid of Mercy's coffin, running to Tay's aid. With the ghost distracted I saw my chance to escape and scrambled to my feet and ran to the church on the hill, desperately searching for a hiding place.

I charged through the church doors and ducked behind a pew, catching my breath. The church was dark except for the faint scraps of light from the street lamps coming in through the east windows, and the air was musty and old, like the air of an antique shop or a scarcely visited natural history museum, and having grown up with an old woman, I had visited my fair share of both places. As I crouched behind the pews I could see the cobwebs hidden underneath them, and the dust that coated the windowsills. It suddenly dawned on me that the doors of the church had been unlocked, and I could see why; it seemed like no one ever used the little building anymore.

I snuck over to a window and peaked through the glass to check on Tay and Taylor. I was hoping to see that the spirit had calmed down and evaporated, and it was safe for me to grab the skull and leave. But as I slowly peered over the grossly dusty windowsill, my heart dropped. The ghost had noticed I was gone, and was speeding towards the church, glaring right at me. I screamed and fell backwards, then began frantically searching the walls and floor, scrambling for some other exit. But there wasn't one, there just wasn't.

Tay caught a glimpse of me through the window from across the graveyard.

"Lori, look out!" he yelled, just as the spirit flung open the church doors with a forceful gust of wind. "She's coming! The vampire's coming!"

I was frozen in terror, fully expecting to have my neck snapped or a set of fiery claws raked across my chest. Yet the ghost stopped dead in her tracks at the sound of Tay's warning, the fury gone from her face. It had been replaced with... Sadness? Shock? Regret?

"I'm not a vampire," she said, her voice quiet.

I recognized her dress now as a less decayed version of the one Mercy's skeleton had been wearing. Underneath the scars and scabs and blood, I could see the remnants of a face that was once gentle and pretty, with big eyes and thin lips. I couldn't believe I didn't register her identity before, it was obvious. She was Mercy Brown.

I tried to say something, but I was scared out of my mind and couldn't think. The only sound I could get my voice to make was a long, low, "uhhhhhhhh..."

I tried to remember what Grandma had told me about public speaking and making phone calls: *Slow down, honey. Take the time to plan your words.*

"I know, Mercy," I said, "I know."

Her eyes locked with mine, and I became aware of a deep sadness within them, a deep feeling of loss. "You do?"

"Of... of course!" I said. She stared at me, wanting a longer answer. I wasn't sure what to say. She really truly did look like some kind of monster. I was still shaking with fear, terrified that if I didn't speak up quickly enough or said the wrong thing, Mercy would turn violent on me again.

I reached up and tapped the corners of my mouth. "You've got... you... no fangs," I said meekly, fumbling for the right answer. "I know, um, I-I know what happened to you, and, but..."

Mercy sank into the pew across from me and let out a long sigh. Taylor and Tay were advancing on the church doors, breathing hard.

Taylor called out to me. "Lori! Are you—"

Mercy raised a hand and the doors slammed shut in front of them. They banged on the wood, trying to force their way in.

"So, you see me as a vampire, do you?" Mercy asked. It wasn't threatening, if anything, she sounded sad.

"I-I, you look, I—"

I cut myself off, took another breath, and counted to five.

"I know you weren't one in life, but, but you have blood on your dress. You sort of look like you could be a vampire. B-but I know you aren't!"

Mercy snickered and crossed her arms. "I bet I look horrible to you." Her expression hardened.

"I didn't want to be remembered this way," Mercy said, her eyes focused on the floor in front of her. "I didn't want my family to die. *I* didn't want to die. They blamed me, and I did nothing wrong. And now my only legacy is my death. That's all I'm remembered for. How I died."

It saddened me to hear her say that, but she seemed to be very much correct. I hadn't heard her name at all before this quest.

She glanced up from the floor, looking straight into my eyes. "Do you know what I wanted? I wanted to be a poet. I was going to be the next Poe or Dickinson. I was going to marry Josiah Walton from church and then move to Boston with him. And he'd get rich as a merchant and I'd stay home and care for our children and cats and I'd write all day."

I could see the tears welling up in her ghostly eyes now, as she remembered the forgotten dream, "But I never got that. All I got was blame. And now I'm remembered as a monster." She turned away.

"A... a poet?" I asked.

"Willows weep within the forest/Clouds drift and spin across the sky/Roses grow within the thorn bush/ I wish I hadn't said goodbye," she recited the stanza as if she'd said it a thousand times before, and maybe in death, she had.

"You wrote that?" I asked, "It's beautiful. You're a fantastic poet." I wouldn't have considered the poem to be anything but mediocre under normal circumstances, but the way Mercy had said it like it was all she still owned gave it an added sense of worth.

I felt for her, I really did. She had had her whole life planned out ahead of her, kind of like I did. We had very different dreams, yes, but I knew how I would feel if my life was cut short before I could become a nurse like Grandma. I would feel like I hadn't really gotten a chance to live. And in my current situation, not getting to go and accomplish that goal was a real possibility.

Tay and Taylor were trying to break the windows now, trying to save me from what they thought must have been a deadly situation. I caught their eyes and raised a hand. *I'm okay*, I mouthed.

"Mercy," I began, "what happened to you wasn't fair. And you didn't deserve it. And I'm sorry we dug up your grave."

Her face turned fiery again as she eyed the skull sitting under the pew. I spoke quickly.

"Listen, this is going to sound crazy, but we need it. We're lost, sort of, and we can't get home, but a man told us he could help us if we stole some things for him, and he wanted this." I gestured to the skull. Mercy studied me in silent thought. It made me uncomfortable, and I felt the need to start rambling.

"I can— we can— I have the shirt from the—" Mercy raised a hand and cut me off. She sighed.

"Alright. Take it. It doesn't do me any good now." She stood and drifted towards the church doors, but something felt wrong.

"Mercy?" I said.

She stopped with her hand resting on the door handle, but she didn't turn around. "Maybe it's too late now," I told her, "but I'll remember you as a poet."

It only happened for a moment, and it was gone in a flicker, a change in the light, but somehow, for a second as Mercy smiled over her shoulder, the blood and scars and rot that marred her face were gone. I saw her as a young, vibrant woman, with a beautiful face and sparkling eyes. I saw Mercy Brown as she had lived. But she turned away from me quickly, the church doors flung open, and she evaporated into thin air. Tay and Taylor burst into the room and ran over to me.

"Lori! Lori, are you okay?" Tay demanded.

"What happened? Where did she go?" Taylor asked.

"I don't know," I said, "but she let me have this." I picked up the skull and handed it to him. Both boys sighed with relief.

"I don't know where she went, but I want to rebury the rest of body as best as we can. She's had a rough afterlife." And with that, I walked out of the church to find my shovel.

PAST

I explained what had happened to Tay and Taylor as we shoveled dirt back into the ground. We were all quiet for a while after I finished.

"A poet, huh?" Tay said, examining the headstone.

"I guess I never thought of what her life was like," Taylor remarked, "I mean, I thought about the vampire thing, but that was it. Sometimes you forget that people from the past were, well, people."

His phrasing wasn't perfect, but I understood exactly what Taylor meant. It was hard to imagine that every marker in this graveyard represented a person, a person who had family, friends, hopes, dreams, and feelings. They had lived, they had died, and they had been forgotten.

It really was dark now, with stars shining and an almost full moon glowing in the sky. After I bandaged Taylor's split chin, we finished covering the grave and packed up our things, deciding to leave the shovels behind. We sprayed an orange with what Taylor had starting calling "The Mothman Juice" and then headed towards the little boutique hotel we had seen downtown. Tay wrapped Mercy's skull in the useless bloody T-shirt from my backpack so he wouldn't have to look at it while he held it. I think he was hoping to forget what he was carrying was a piece of human remains. Mothman couldn't get to us fast enough.

We waited for him outside a cafe near the hotel so that he wouldn't have to bust through a wall to get to us. Mothman didn't really seem like the type to knock. We took some hot teas and bagels from the inside of the cafe, then sat at a dainty little periwinkle table and chair set on the sidewalk.

I nibbled at my bagel, tasting the sweet hints of cinnamon baked into the dough, but somehow I wasn't very hungry anymore. I couldn't stop thinking about Mercy, and the dream she never got the chance to realize. What if I ended up like her? What if I, too, died young? Or worse, somehow failed to complete my nursing degree and ended up working a minimum wage job until I turned seventy and living alone in a tiny motel room with eight cats and—

"Lori?" Taylor said. He and Tay were staring at me with puzzled frowns and raised eyebrows. "Are you okay?"

I looked down at my tea. I was tempted to just say that yes, I was fine, thank you very much, like I had become so used to telling everyone else who asked that question in the week since Grandma died. But for some reason, I told them the truth.

"It's just... I've been thinking about Mercy, and how she never got what she really wanted out of life. What if that happens to us? What if we don't make it out of here?"

Tay sighed. "You keep mentioning that you need to go home. What's waiting for you there?"

I was taken aback. Was he saying that he *didn't* need to go home? "I... just, well, life, I guess. I've got plans and dreams."

"Of course, but is there something urgent? Do you have someone waiting for you?" Taylor asked.

I had to laugh. "Well, sort of. My cousin was supposed to take me to live with her this morning. My grandma just died and she was my legal guardian. But other than that I don't have any family or anything."

I took a sip of my tea and realized that the table had gone quiet. Tay looked shocked, and Taylor seemed just a little bit horrified. It dawned on me that I had just casually revealed something incredibly personal and tragic. I felt odd to be talking this much, especially to be talking about myself.

Taylor looked like he was about to say something, probably the usual *Oh, I'm so sorry to hear that* or *She's in a better place now* or *Things will get better with time* that I'd been hearing non-stop since the funeral. But anyone who's ever lost someone important to them will tell you that you can only hear things like that so often before they stop helping, before they take on a sad, sad irony because you know that anyone who says this to you has no idea what you're going through really and probably never will. I cut Taylor off, not wanting to hear any of that from someone I was coming to respect.

"I don't know, what's waiting for you guys?" I said.

Tay snorted. "Absolutely nothing."

Taylor rubbed his arm and looked away. "I don't think anybody's looking for me, if that's what you mean."

Taylor seemed sad about this, like the topic was somehow a sore subject for him, but I didn't understand why that would be. I took a risk and prodded him further.

"What do you mean? Surely you don't live alone."

"No," he said, "it's kind of funny you mentioned your parents didn't raise you. Mine didn't either. I live in a group home type place; I guess you could say. I have foster parents, but we're not close."

"Oh," I had assumed that both my companions had had families to go back to, because that was what every other kid I knew had. Growing up, I had always been the odd one out. Sure, some kids had parents that were divorced or they had a single mom, but no one else was an orphan.

"What happened to your parents? Both of your parents," Tay asked, looking to me.

"They died in a car crash when I was about six months old," I informed him, and judging from his expression, I delivered the news too nonchalantly yet again. What could I do? I'd been repeating the same story all my life. "I don't really remember them, though. I've lived with my grandma for almost all my life."

"That's rough," Tay said, "I'm sorry."

"It's okay," I said quickly, "I mean, it's not okay as in it's fine that my parents died, because it's not, but it's not something that's left me too emotionally scarred or anything. If I could have them *not* die in a car crash, then I would, but it's just the way things worked out. My grandma took great care of me. I loved her a lot."

I felt like crying all of a sudden; the wound from losing my grandma still so fresh. At times, it had felt like she was my real mom. Tay looked to Taylor for his answer.

"My mom was fifteen when she had me, and she didn't know who my dad was. She didn't want me. I was never adopted. So I live in a group home." He bit his lip. I almost expected him to start crying, but his face was blank, apathetic, numb. I reached across the table and took his hand in mine.

"Taylor, I... I'm sorry," I whispered. I didn't really know what else to tell him. What can you say to make a situation like that any better? Nothing.

Tay reached over and awkwardly patted Taylor's shoulder.

"Damn, that's rough," he said. "but if it makes you feel any better, I live in one too."

I stared at him in shock. *None* of us had parents?

"What hap— why?" I stuttered.

Tay chuckled and looked up at the stars. "I lived with my folks till I was four, but they got into drugs. I mean, really hard stuff. It was dangerous, I remember playing with used needles a couple of times. Anyway, somebody called CPS, and off I went. I haven't seen 'em since I was seven." He got a faraway look in his eyes, remembering.

Again, I was left speechless. I had never met anyone with parents like Tay's, that kind of thing just didn't happen to kids who went to private girls' schools in Concord, New Hampshire. I thought about what that must have been like for him, with strange people coming into his house and taking him away from his parents forever. Going away to a new home at only four years old. He must have had to learned to fend for himself at a very young age.

I looked at the two boys sitting across from me, my respect for both of them increased a thousand times over. Most people I talked to told me my life was bad, but I had nothing on them.

"Tay?" Taylor said meekly. "That's rough."

We laughed, and Tay gave him a playful shove in the ribs.

"But in all seriousness," I said, "I'm sorry you both had to go through that."

"Well, it's just like you said," Tay said, "it's just the way things worked out for us. Nothing we can do to change it."

"But you'll be out of there in a few years, right? Then what will you do? Do you have, like, a college fund or something?" They both shook their heads.

"I've run away a few times," Tay said, "lived off the streets for a few nights. It wasn't bad. Someday I'll probably just take my guitar and go. I'll play for money until I make it big."

That was an alien career plan to me. Even though I was only fifteen, I already had a college fund, a strict SAT prep schedule, a list of schools I was going to apply to. And Tay was going to enter adulthood like a whirlwind, just leave home whenever he saw fit and struggle to make his own way in the world. I could see a million things that were wrong with his plan, and a million reasons why he shouldn't go through with it, and a million ways he could end up dead before he turned 20, and I had a million questions for him, but all I could bring myself to say was, "You play guitar?"

He smiled. "Oh, yeah. Piano, too. I started learning when I was in first grade, it was the only thing that kept me sane. If we can find an instrument somewhere I'll play for you guys."

"What do you play?" Taylor asked.

"Anything," Tay said, making a sweeping motion with his hand. "Bach, The Beatles, The Rocky Horror Picture Show. And if I don't know it, I could probably learn it within the hour." He laughed again. "Anyway, enough about me. What do you want to do, Taylor?"

"I'm not really sure," he said, "but probably art or something. I like colors." That brought a smile to my face. Taylor was so creative, if he didn't become an artist it would be the world's loss, not his.

"What about you, Lori?" he asked.

"I'm going to be a nurse," I said with pride, as I always did when talking about my dream job. "Just like my Grandma was! She worked for—"

Before I could finish my sentence, a loud "SCREEEEEEEEE!!!" cut through the air as Mothman landed beside our table. I had stupidly left the orange on the sidewalk under one of the table legs, and Mothman flipped the entire table out of the way to get to it, sending hot tea, bagels, and the periwinkle piece of furniture flying into the wall of the cafe.

"SCREEEEEEEE!!!" He grabbed the orange and flew into the air, squatting on the roof of the cafe and eating the fruit like it was corn on the cob. The three of us sat in stunned silence for a moment, but as soon as we made eye contact we all burst out laughing. What else could we do? It's not every day a giant half-man half-moth flips over your dinner table.

Tay patted the skull in his lap, still wrapped in the T-shirt. "Alright, I guess we should give him this and text Drake."

Mothman descended from the roof top and approached us, curiosity and hunger in his big red eyes.

"Screeeee?" he inquired. I noticed that this time he had a drawstring bag on his back. I opened it up and saw a note from Drake: *Bones are fragile. Mothman's grip is strong. Please put the skull in here. ~ Drake.*

We put the skull into Drake's bag, threw in my bloody shirt for extra padding (and because I couldn't reuse it anyways), and closed the bag as tight as we could. Tay texted Drake to let him know we were ready, and then Mothman was off, scree-ing with excitement.

"Well," Tay said, "are you all ready to turn in for the night?"

We walked off to the hotel, laughing and joking the whole way. My shyness had evaporated like magic, and Tay's temper and Taylor's quirkiness didn't worry me anymore. Despite the fact that I had just dug up a grave and seen a ghost and lost my tea to an overeager Mothman and the fact that I was literally farther away from home than I'd ever been before in my life, it was the first time since Grandma died that I felt truly happy.

HOPE

Brrrrrrring! Brrrrrrrrrrring!

I could hear our flip phone ringing and buzzing from somewhere on the hotel floor. It was early morning, with the sun not yet risen. Tay, Taylor, and I dozed under piles of blankets on the floor again while a woman in the real layer occupied the bed. Tay groaned and rolled over, thumping his hand on the floor in search of the phone in the darkness. He found it, but only after a good twenty seconds or so. He rolled over again and held it to his ear.

"Hello?... Yeah, we got it ok. No injuries." I had forgotten that we hadn't called Drake yet. Tay was silent for a little while, listening to Drake's instructions in the darkness.

"Ok, I'll ask," he said. "Hey, Taylor, Lori, are you awake?"

"Yes," I said, sitting up. Taylor grunted from across the room.

"Awesome," Tay said, "you guys wanna steal the Hope Diamond?"

"The Hope Diamond?" I asked. I was shocked that our next mission was something I'd actually heard of before, and surprised that Drake would trust us to find something so famous. "You mean, *the* Hope Diamond? The one at the Smithsonian?"

Tay snorted. "No, the one in Budapest," he said. I reached over and tried to smack him in the ribs, but I missed in the darkness and just kind of swatted his neck instead.

"Ow," Taylor mumbled, "what are you guys doing over there?"

"Well?" I heard Drake's gruff voice over the phone.

"Yeah, we'll do it," Tay said. Drake told him something else I couldn't hear, then Tay bid him farewell and flipped the phone shut.

"Alright, guess we'd better catch a flight to DC," he said.

Taylor stood up, stretched, and opened the curtains, but it was still very dark outside. I checked the clock. It was 4 in the morning. "Why was Drake calling us so late?" I asked. "It's one a.m. in Las Vegas."

"Dunno," Tay said, "but we don't have to get up yet, do we?"

And with that, he pulled his blanket back over his body and shut his eyes. Taylor followed suit, slinking back to his makeshift mattress. I laid back down too, and before I knew it, I was asleep.

*****

When I woke up again, the clock read 9:16, and Tay and Taylor still lay unmoving under their blankets. I went into the bathroom to change clothes. Ironically enough, the T-shirt from Drake was from the Washington Monument. I put it on, brushed my hair and teeth, and went to wake up the boys.

Taylor woke up the moment I put my hand on his shoulder, his eyes opening in an instant.

"Hey, um, time to get up," I said.

He stood up and walked to the bathroom to start getting ready, instantly and fully awake. I wished that I could be that much of a morning person. Waking up Tay wasn't as easy, and I had to shake him a few times.

"Five more minutes," he mumbled.

"Come on," I said, "we're waiting on you."

He reluctantly dragged himself out from underneath the blankets and started helping me pack our stuff while he waited for Taylor to finish up in the bathroom.

After we had all gotten ready, we walked down to the hotel lobby for breakfast and to draft a game plan.

"Alright," Tay said, fully awake now. "The airport is a little far from here, but the highway isn't. We can just do our little hitchhike thingy again until we get to Providence."

Providence. The word made my stomach drop, because I knew that was where I was going to end up once all of this was over. I still wasn't looking forward to it, and being in that city was just going to make me sad and anxious.

It's going to be okay, I tried to tell myself, *you're just going to the airport. You'll barely even see the city. Then you'll be in Washington in no time.* The thoughts weren't as calming as I wanted them to be, but what could I do? It was the closest airport there was. We finished eating, and then we began our trek to the highway.

It was about an hour of walking, but we made it to an entrance ramp, and hopped into a little red Volkswagen with a man driving and a woman in the passenger seat. The three of us, plus our large backpacks, were crammed into the tiny backseat, and to make matters worse, the couple were fighting.

"You never listen to me!" cried the man. "You just ignore every single thing I have to say!"

"Well, maybe if you said anything worthwhile, *Michael*—"

"Don't you talk to me like that!"

"What do you mean, *don't you talk to me like that!* You talk to me like that all day long!"

"If you bothered to listen to me, then you'd know that wasn't true!"

"Damn, Michael," Tay said.

Taylor wasn't listening. Instead, he was drawing patterns with his foot in the dirty beige carpet of the car.

"Are you ok?" I asked him.

"Yeah," he said, "I just don't like when people fight, is all."

I could see where he was coming from. Michael and his wife didn't even know we were in their car, but you could feel the tension of their argument from a mile away. I decided it would be good to distract ourselves.

"Okay," I said, "we don't have to listen to them. Do you want to play a game?"

Taylor seemed surprised at my offer.

"Sure," he said, "what should we do?"

I thought for a moment. "Do you know about the alphabet game? Where you try to find a word that starts with each letter of the alphabet on the road signs?"

Taylor smiled. "Okay," he said, "let's try it."

We searched for the letter A as the couple in front of us fought on, and we found it on one of those brown ATTRACTION signs pointing to the exit for a museum. The letter B was on a semi-truck next to us, and a gas station near the road started with C. Soon Tay was playing too, and we got up to the letter G before our drivers drove off an exit ramp. We got out of their car, thankful to be away from the bickering couple, and hopped in a silver minivan with two sleeping kids in the backseat and a much happier couple in front. We squeezed ourselves into the wayback of the car and continued playing. Our luck was good enough that this family was going to the airport too, and we rode in their car the rest of the way there. We got to the airport in less than an hour, with only the letter Z left to find.

We found the flight schedule, and made plans to get on a plane to DC that left in two hours. We wandered around the terminal for a while, still looking for that Z.

"Dang," Tay said, "if only this airport had a zoo."

"Maybe we can find a zone of some sort," Taylor said, "like a construction zone or a smoking-free zone."

"Or maybe some zombies," I added.

We didn't end up finding that Z, but we did pick up some sandwiches for lunch. We ate on the floor by the gate to our flight, watching the people go by.

"Anybody been to DC before?" Tay asked. "I haven't."

"I went for a field trip in eighth grade," I said.

"Really?" Taylor said, "my school had one of those too, but it was kind of expensive, so I didn't go."

"Oh," I said, recalling Taylor's less than fortunate parental situation.

"What did you see there?" Tay asked me.

"A lot! The Jefferson and Lincoln memorials, Arlington National Cemetery, and the zoo. We saw the Capitol and the White House but we didn't go in. We spent a lot of time at the Smithsonian, actually. I saw the Hope Diamond."

"It's kind of weird Drake is sending us after something so famous," Taylor remarked.

"Yeah, didn't he mention there's only one of every special object for all the layers?" Tay said. "I'm sure the Warrens lose stuff all the time in a basement like that, and nobody's going to be digging up Mercy Brown anytime soon. But if we take this diamond, people are definitely going to notice. Like, a lot of people."

I thought about that for a moment. The people in the organic layer would have no way of explaining what had happened. The diamond would just be gone, with no signs of anyone breaking into the museum and no damage done to the display case. It would be there one moment, and gone the next. And because it was such a famous, priceless gemstone, the media would be all over the case.

"It's going to be a mess in the human layer," I said. Then, another thought entered my mind. "Wait, isn't this artifact supposed to be really cursed? Like, everyone who touches it dies?"

"I don't think it's gotten quite to *that* point," Taylor said, "but a lot of its owners did end up seriously injured or dead, if I remember correctly."

"Fun," Tay muttered.

"We shouldn't have to touch it for very long, though," Taylor continued, "Mothman can do all that for us."

"Yeah, I guess so," I said, but I wasn't quite comforted. Mothman was a little klutzy at times, and if something went wrong...

The flight attendant came on the loud speaker and announced that our flight was boarding. We threw away our sandwich wrappers and got on the plane, hoping for the best.

The flight wasn't quite full this time, and we managed to find a row of seats all to ourselves. Taylor was at the window seat, I was in the middle, and Tay sat by the aisle. He tried to sleep during the flight while Taylor kept looking out the window, even after we had soared above the clouds and there wasn't much to look at anymore. I pointed this out to him, and he said, "Oh, I know, I just like looking at the colors."

I looked out the window, trying to see the world the way he did, but I couldn't tell what was so interesting to him. "I see white and blue," I said flatly.

"Yes," he responded, "but there are lots of different shades of them."

Um, okay. He wasn't wrong, but it wasn't like looking at a rainbow or anything.

"I have kind of a thing for colors," he said, "have you heard of synesthesia?" I shook my head no. "It's a mental condition I have. It means I associate noises with colors."

"What do you mean by that?" I asked him.

"Like, when I hear something, a color pops up in my head. Your voice is lavender. Tay's is navy." He clapped his hands. "That was bright yellow."

"Oh," I said, "that's... that's fun. It's... different, but fun."

"It can be annoying sometimes, though," he said, "like when I'm trying to listen to music but the colors clash."

"God, I would hate that," Tay said. I jumped in my seat, startled. I hadn't realized he was listening.

The plane landed about an hour after that, and right as we walked into the airport, we got a call from Drake. Tay dug the phone out of his jeans pocket and answered it. "Hello?"

"Tay. Taylor. Lori. Don't go after the diamond tonight," Drake gasped, frantic and out of breath. I heard Mothman screeing in the background.

"Why? What's wrong?" I asked.

"You remember the man I told you about? The one who started all this and brought us into the sublayers?" I did, but barely. Drake hadn't told us a whole lot about him, but I knew anyone so reckless wasn't our ally.

"I've gotten word from my trio of spies that he's after the Hope Diamond too, and he has werewolves guarding the stone. It's a full moon tonight. You can't go after the diamond until tomorrow. I've sent two sets of trios after his trail, so you shouldn't have to deal with him, at least not this time. But it won't be totally safe until after the full moon, until after the werewolf danger passes," Drake spat out the words at an incredible speed, it almost sounded like he was talking in another language.

"Uh, okay then," Tay said.

"If you think we're in danger, we won't do it," Taylor said.

"Good. Thank you," Drake said.

"Drake, we're already in Washington, DC. Are we still safe? Is there anything else we should do until tomorrow?" I asked.

"No, you should be completely safe during the day, but stay away from the natural history museum, *especially* once nightfall hits. Just take a break today. See the city, get some sleep. I'll update you if I hear anything else." He hung up without saying goodbye.

"Okay," Tay said as he slid the phone back into his pocket. "I guess we aren't getting the diamond today."

"Werewolves, huh?" Taylor remarked, "I didn't think of those. I didn't know people still believed in them."

"And we haven't heard much about the man who brought us here." I said, thinking aloud. It was strange to think of him, this elusive man with half a chupacabra's head for a face, the man whose unstoppable grief and selfishness had forced me into a strange new reality. I had to wonder if my own grief over Grandma could ever cause me to do something so completely crazy...

"Well, what are we going to do today?" Tay asked, "Lori, you said you'd been here. What's good?"

I thought for a moment. We had a whole day to ourselves to just explore the nation's capital, completely immune to lines and crowds and cars and even laws.

"Well…" I said, "we can see pretty much anything we want; there's no one around to stop us. We can always just head downtown and wing it from there, almost everything's within walking distance."

"Alrighty," Tay said, "let's hop in a car."

Finding a ride to the city was much easier this time, because the street was lined with taxis waiting to take tourists to their hotels. We climbed into the backseat of a random one, and the man in the passenger seat told the driver his hotel was just a few blocks away from the National Mall. Perfect.

We arrived at his hotel, a quaint four story white building in the heart of the city. To our glee, it was right between two awesome looking museums: The International Spy Museum, and the Museum of Crime and Punishment.

"Is it just me being weird," Taylor asked, "or are you guys really, really curious about those?"

"Dude, I don't even like museums, and *I* want to go in," Tay said.

I hadn't seen these on my school trip, and I was surprised such museums even existed at all. But I supposed after the Warren's Occult Museum, I really shouldn't have questioned the kind of topics that were museum-worthy.

We went into the spy museum first, and it was awesome to be able to skip the line out front. We went up the elevator to the second floor to find galleries filled with secret documents, tiny cameras hidden in everyday objects, and disguises of all types. The exhibits reminded me of Drake telling us about his own spy trios, but something told me the spies Drake trained didn't get to use guns disguised as umbrellas and tape recorders hidden in nickels.

We found an interactive display on code cracking and tried it. Taylor was surprisingly talented at it, getting a higher score than Tay and I combined. He would have done even better, but then a little boy in the real layer came along and started using the same interactive, making it hard to differentiate between our game and the shadow of the one in the real world because they overlapped.

We wandered around the museum for about two hours, ogling over the artifacts and trying the few displays that weren't being used in the real world. It was cool, but I wasn't so sure I'd want to be a spy myself. The consequences of getting caught were a little too dire, according to an informational passage on the wall.

We crossed the street without looking both ways and entered the crime museum.

The lobby of the museum had another line of tourists at the ticket counter, but it was definitely much less crowded than the spy museum. Yellow police tape covered the windows, and mugshots of famous criminals dotted the walls. When we first walked in the door, we saw a bullet-riddled car sitting in the main hall.

Taylor examined it closely and pointed to the information card sitting beside it. "Look, it was Bonnie and Clyde's escape car," he said.

"Wow, that's actually awesome," Tay said. He reached over and ran his fingertips over the bullet holes in the driver's side door.

"Tay, this is a museum! You're not supposed to touch anything," I chided.

He turned to look at me and scoffed.

"In the real world, no," he said, "but it doesn't hurt anything if we touch it here. Nobody to stop us, remember?"

I had been more concerned about the preservation of the artifact. Though Tay and Taylor had no way of knowing this, my own father had been a museum curator before he died, and because of that I cared more than the average person about keeping museums in good shape. But he was still right, anything we could do to this car wouldn't affect the real layer's artifact in the slightest.

Tay leaned against the car and folded his arms across his chest.

"Do I look like a badass yet?" he asked Taylor. We all laughed.

"But really, though," Tay said, "we should find a camera. Imagine the photo ops in this place."

"That's a great idea!" Taylor proclaimed. He ran off into a crowd of tourists. He came back a few moments later with a sleek black camera around his neck, taken from a large man in a Hawaiian shirt and cargo shorts.

"Perfect," Tay said.

He did his "badass" pose again, and Taylor snapped the shot. Tay looked at his photo on the display screen and laughed.

"Oh my god, that's great, that's so great!" He said with all the excitement of a nerdy eighth grade girl at an anime convention.

"But you know what would be even better..." he put his hand on the car handle to the front seat and pulled. The door opened.

Tay turned to us, open mouthed. "No way!" he cried, stepping over the black ropes around the car and getting into the driver's seat. "No-o-o-o way!"

He turned to me, his face lit up like a little kid on Christmas. "Lori, get in the passenger seat," he said.

"What? No! They probably died in there!" I said.

"Oh, come on, it'll look so cool! We'll be Bonnie and Clyde!"

I hesitated. I would never, ever touch something like this in the real world.

"Just one picture," Tay said, seeing the worried look on my face. "Please?"

He gave me the sweetest smile he could muster. This was probably the happiest I'd ever seen him. Maybe the happiest I'd ever get to see him.

Forgive me, Grandma, I thought before climbing into the seat beside Tay. "Yeah!" He cried.

He but his feet up on the dashboard and smirked into the camera. I didn't know how to pose.

"Don't smile, just, like, look smug. Yeah! Just like that! Exactly!" He instructed me.

After Taylor took the picture, we got out of the car to see it. Tay was right, we did look really cool. He squealed with excited and skipped to the staircase.

"Come on!" he said. "Maybe they'll have something from Al Capone!"

We had a great time in the museum, trying the displays, looking behind glass cases, and getting a little too close to the artifacts. And, of course, taking lots of pictures. We pretended we were cowboys in the western crime exhibit, knights in the medieval torture chamber, and gangsters in Chicagoland.

"Aw man, I hope we get to go there next," Tay said as we went through the exhibits on the Chicago mob. "Now that's a cool city."

Both boys seemed to be having the times of their lives, with Tay geeking out over all the stuff from famous criminals and Taylor finding the best poses for us and talking in funny accents that he changed to match the section of the museum we were in. He was having a ball with the whole pretending thing, you could just tell.

We eventually meandered our way downstairs to a CSI exhibit. A fake body lie splayed across a table, and evidence from the crime was plastered all over the walls, challenging the visitor to solve the murder, like a real life FBI case.

"Alright, Agent Scully," Taylor said to Tay as we wandered over to the body. "Who did this? Or should I say... what did this?"

"How come I'm Scully? Why not Mulder?" Tay asked.

"Because you're more of a skeptic. I, on the other hand, want to believe."

"What makes you say that? You've known me three days."

"I've changed my mind. Lori's Scully."

"I'm what?" I asked.

"Wait, now why is she Scully?" Tay asked.

"Because she's a girl."

"So I'm Mulder now."

"No, I'm Mulder. You can be an alien or something."

"Hey!"

I still had no idea what they were arguing about, but it was silly. I walked over to a display game. "Come on, I want to try this. You can both be Scully."

"Mulder," they both said at once.

"That too."

We finished the museum shortly after that. We collected a barrage of pictures and killed three whole hours. We stopped to get dinner at a burger joint near the museum, then walked down to the national mall to see the typical touristy stuff: The Washington Monument, the Capitol Building, the White House. It was getting late, so we didn't go into any of them, but I was glad Tay and Taylor at least got to see them. The way they lived in the real layer, I wasn't sure if they'd ever get a chance to come back.

We sprawled out on the lawn below the Washington Monument, looking up at the impossibly tall obelisk and watching the sun go down.

"Today," Tay declared, "was great. You guys," he pointed to me and Taylor. "Are great."

"Ditto," Taylor whispered, watching the sky in awe.

"How many colors are up there?" I asked him.

He sighed contentedly, like a well-loved dog just before it falls asleep. "Tons."

I smiled. I couldn't help but do anything else.

Suddenly, as the sun finally set, and the stars were just barely twinkling into existence in the sky, something odd happened. For a moment, instead of seeing the monuments and museums lighting up one by one, bright white against the increasing darkness around them, I saw a vision of Taylor.

He was younger, smaller, but it was still definitely him, with his lanky limbs, golden hair, and child-like face. He ran around a green space decorated with giant tan concrete turtles, the park separated from hundreds of cars speeding down a highway by only a chain link-fence. He chased after an older girl with long dark curly hair, the both of them laughing. The girl sped over to a giant snapping turtle, about 5 feet tall and the length of a limousine, put her hands on its rounded shell, and vaulted herself to the top of it. Taylor paused at the place she had jumped, trying to catch his breath.

"Lanie! Taylor! Time to go! It'll be dark soon!" The voice of a tall woman called out to the children from the edge of the playground.

She sat on a much smaller tortoise, her figure just a black silhouette against the quickly fading sunlight.

"One minute!" called the girl, Lanie.

She looked down at Taylor, who held up his arms. He squealed with excitement as she picked him up and put him down on the turtle's shell. Then,

"Whoa."

Little Taylor gasped at all he could see. There were colors everywhere. Colors painted across the sky by the setting sun, colors coming and going as cars raced down the freeway, and colors hidden in the endless sea of green trees that obscured the south end of the zoo. It would have been a mundane sight to most people; the filth of the highway, the short range of vision caused by the short height of the turtle. But to Taylor, as he stood with his head held high on the back of a giant reptile, he saw a rainbow, and he was on top of the world.

Suddenly the vision was gone, and I snapped back to the present. I was back in DC, next to Tay and a normal-sized, 15-year-old Taylor, watching the sun set and the sky grow dark.

I looked to Taylor, then to Tay, both of whom still gazed up at the sky like nothing had happened. They probably hadn't seen my vision, then, because if it had been shared by the three of us, surely one of them would have stirred. Somebody certainly would have said something, right? But just to be sure...

"Did either of you see that? Taylor and the turtles?"

Taylor turned his head to stare at me blankly.

Tay scoffed. "Um, see what?"

So it hadn't been a weird, you-three-are-all-connected-here thing. What I saw for some reason came to me and me alone.

"I... um, never mind. I thought I saw some weird shapes in the clouds."

Taylor sat up to examine the sky more closely. "Oh! Which ones?"

"They're gone now. Uh, sorry."

"Oh." Taylor sank back down into the grass.

I shook my head, trying to clear the vision from my mind. Whatever it had been, it hadn't harmed anyone, right? It was just a cute memory from when Taylor was small.

"We should probably start walking back to the hotel. It'll be dark soon," I said. Whatever I had seen, I figured it was best to move on and try to let it go.

*****

We meandered our way back to the hotel, stopping to take more pictures in front of the monuments and museums and any other mildly interesting things we saw. Taylor squatting beside a pigeon. Me peeking out from a building shaped like an octagon. Tay dancing with a statue of Einstein.

We had just made our way back to the spy museum when Tay stopped and said, "Wait. Did we ever get a picture of all three of us?"

I looked at Taylor. He shrugged. We had taken so many photos throughout the day, I had lost track.

"Well, let's get one!" Tay said. His face lit up with an idea, and he reached a hand into his pocket. "Does the cell phone have a camera? Hey, it does! Let's get one on here and send it to Drake."

We crowded under the neon red SPY sign over the museum and snapped a picture of all of us smiling at the camera, arms around each other, the neon from the sign casting a bright red light over us. It was a simple picture, but it was perfect. Tay sent it to Drake with no caption and we finally entered the hotel lobby and followed a woman into her room.

As we were pulling the blankets onto the floor, the phone buzzed in Tay's pocket. He pulled it out, opened it up, and laughed. Drake had sent us a selfie of his own, a photo of him squatting and making a peace sign with his fingers beside a sleeping Mothman, who was curled up like a dog on the overstuffed couch in his office. We all fell to the floor, laughing ourselves silly. It was good to know that Drake had a sense of humor.

I pulled my blankets over my neck, perfectly content for the second night in a row. A new record.

The woman in the real layer turned out the lights. Taylor nestled under his nest of blankets a few feet to my right, and Tay relaxed with his arms folded underneath his head to my left, contentedly gazing at the ceiling fan.

"Good night, Taylor. Good night, Tay."

"Good night," Taylor said.

"Good night," Tay said.

I was tempted to add an *I love you* afterword, but I thought they might not like that. We'd only known each other for three days. But somehow, they felt like my best friends, like they'd been a part of me forever. Some part of me really did want to love them.

I finally fell asleep after what had felt like one of the best days of my life, for once unafraid of what tomorrow might bring.

*****

We woke up at about 9:30 the next morning with a message from Drake. *Call me*, it read.

"Okay, then," Tay said, punching Drake's number into the phone. "That's not ominous at all..."

"Change of plans," Drake said as soon as he answered our call. "Don't go after the diamond until after the museum closes." We looked at each other, confused.

"Okay," Tay said, "but why?"

"Too many people are in the museum. There's only one Hope Diamond for all the layers, so when you steal the diamond, they won't see you run into the room break the glass, they'll just see that the diamond was there one moment and completely vanished the next. That will cause too much confusion and chaos. But if you take the diamond after the museum closes, it will look more like a robbery. It will still be an extremely mysterious disappearance, and it will cause a media panic, but it won't look so... paranormal," Drake explained.

"But why do we care what the people in the real layer think? We'll still get the diamond," Tay said.

"Yes, but at what cost?" Drake said, "We don't want to create such irrefutable proof of the unexplained. It will cause people to question everything they believe to be true. They'll need an explanation for what happened with the diamond, and who knows what beliefs people will develop? It will cause a massive imbalance in the layers as new beliefs come to the forefront. If people see such a famous artifact as the Hope Diamond just disappearing from its case without a trace, the media storm will be massive, and we just can't predict how it will affect us."

I thought about Drake's words. How would people react to seeing such a feat? I knew it would definitely make me start believing in ghosts.

"Wait, when we stole Mercy's skull, we carried it into a café and no one noticed," Tay remarked.

"When someone in a sublayer is holding onto a universal object, no one in the real layer can see it until it is put down. This is why when Mothman carries artifacts to me, people in the real layer don't see a skull or a doll flying above their heads at a hundred miles per hour."

"Okay, I see what you mean," I said, "but what do we do until then? Do we have another free day?"

"Actually," Drake said, "while you're in town, I did find another set of tasks to assign you to."

"*Set* of tasks?" Tay asked.

"I have a list of less renowned objects in the area that may or may not exist within all layers, but I'm not certain of their validity. I'll give you their names, and you'll move them to see if their real world silhouette appears. If no silhouette is seen, I would like you to send them to me. These objects aren't as powerful as the main ones I am sending you after, and this is why I'm not sure if they are truly universal or not. They also shouldn't be very dangerous, so securing them, if any of them are indeed universal, should be easy. But I'm doubting any of them will be universal. I just need to be certain."

Tay looked to me and Taylor, mouthing, *should we?* Taylor and I nodded. We didn't have anything better to do.

"Ok, we'll do it," Tay said.

"Excellent!" Drake said. "I'll text the list to you. It's about seven or eight objects, just get done what you can. The museum closes at five-thirty." He hung up without saying goodbye.

I read the list that Drake sent us, and he was right, I didn't really think any of these objects would be special, and if they were, I doubted that they'd have very much power. A potentially cursed soup ladle. A brick from a building that seemed to be only mildly haunted at best. A rocking chair haunted by a president, but it was president Woodrow Wilson. They all seemed fairly mediocre at best. But we had told Drake we'd test them out, so we had to honor our promise.

"You guys want to try number four?" Taylor asked. Number four on the list was a place called the exorcist staircase, followed by an address in the Georgetown neighborhood. Drake's instructions told us that since the stairs were concrete, we should just chisel off a corner to test, and chisel off a larger chunk of rock to send him if they were special.

"Sure," I said, "it looks like the ladle is on the way there, too."

Tay gave an annoyed sign and ran his fingers through his hair. "Alright, that's kind of far and my feet are tired. Let's find a ride."

We decided the most reliable way of getting to the stairs was to hop on one of the tour buses that stopped at the spy museum every hour or so, since the tour route was plastered to the side of every bus we knew they stopped near Georgetown. We sat in the back row, away from all the tourists, and waited for all the passengers to stop getting on and off so the bus could start.

Taking the bus turned out to be a better idea than I expected. It only took about forty-five minutes to get to Georgetown, and despite the tour guide's annoying voice and poor jokes, it was a nice way to see more of the city. Taylor sat with his eyes glued to the window the whole time. He was so entranced he didn't notice when someone from the real layer sat down in his seat right on top of him.

Georgetown was a bustling little neighborhood, with modern-day stores and cafes operating out of old fashioned buildings. The haunted soup ladle was located in a museum called the Old Stone

House, and we found the building pretty quickly. It was aptly named, as it was literally an old house made of stone, and it stuck out among the brightly colored facades and window displays of its retail neighbors.

Tay opened the door and we all walked inside the museum lobby. It was a historic home museum, designed to showcase what life in the eighteenth century was like. I wandered over to the fireplace in the adjacent room and found the ladle hanging in front of it.

"Got it!" I called to Tay and Taylor as I grabbed the ladle and moved it around. It left a clear silhouette in the real layer. It was normal; not haunted or cursed or universal at all. Tay and Taylor entered the room, and I wiggled it around some more to show them this.

"Nice," Tay said, "we can go find the staircase now." He and Taylor left the room as I put the ladle back on the mantle. I turned around, but as I did, I could've sworn I saw a face peering down at me from the top of the stairs. I did a double take and it was gone, but I really thought I saw something...

I joined my companions outside the home and we made our way to a hardware store where we picked up three sets of chisels and hammers. We then found what were known as the exorcist stairs. They were a long concrete set of steps between a red brick building and a grey stone wall. A short archway between the wall and building hovered above the upper section of the steps. A plaque explained that the steps had been used the film the final death scene in the movie *The Exorcist*. Lovely.

"Oh yeah, I remember that scene," Tay remarked as he read the plaque. "That movie was freaky."

Taylor sat down and began chiseling at a corner on the bottom of the stairs. "I think it took place near where I live," he told us as he worked. "The real exorcism, I believe."

"The real exorcism? I thought that movie was fake," I said. I'd never seen it because horror movies terrified me, but I knew enough about it to know that the plot was exactly the kind of thing you hope to God is fiction.

"The movie wasn't a documentary or anything, but it was based off a book that was based off a real case. It was a ten-year-old boy. He lived here in DC for a while, but when his family thought he was possessed they went to St. Louis to find a priest. It took a long time and a lot more than a priest, but they saved him from the demon," Taylor explained.

"Oh," I said, sufficiently creeped out for the day. "Wonderful."

I sat down beside him and started chiseling.

"Wasn't the movie cursed, too? I bet that's why Drake sent us here," Tay said.

"That was *Poltergeist* that was cursed," Taylor said.

"Wait, no, I'm thinking of *Amityville Horror*," Tay said.

"Is there any scary movie out there that isn't cursed?" I asked. I was never turning on a TV again. My good Christian granny had always warned me to stay away from this kind of thing.

"I think you should be safe with *Sharknado*," Tay said, "unless you live near an aquarium."

"Ha, ha." I said. I handed him a chisel. "Get to work."

Breaking off a chunk of the staircase took way longer than expected, even with all three of us working at once. Taylor finally got his little corner off, but it only took a couple of hours. Our efforts were wasted; we could still see the little section of staircase he had removed in the real layer, completely unharmed. He dejectedly put the little corner back. It was close to four o'clock now, so we grabbed a quick dinner at a pizza place and walked back to the tour bus stop.

Our ride to the Smithsonian wasn't much different from our ride to Georgetown, only this time we were heading deeper into the heart of the city instead of away from it. The sun was starting to set now, tinting the sky with gentle shades of pink and yellow, and the museums were just starting to close. We hopped off the bus at the Washington Monument and started our trek towards the natural history museum.

"Wait!" Taylor cried. He removed an apple and spritzed it with Mothman's special pink spray.

"What are you doing? We don't have the diamond yet," Tay said.

"Yes, but it'll probably take less than an hour to get it. This way we'll have less time to wait for Mothman and we can make him pick up the diamond instead of one of us so we can avoid the curse," Taylor said.

It was a smart plan. I certainly didn't want to touch that gemstone if I didn't have to.

The Smithsonian was huge, with at least six or seven massive buildings lining the mall. The National Museum of Natural History was one of the biggest.

"Whoa," Taylor said as we entered the lobby of the museum.

Whoa was right. The ceiling of the rotunda was a beautiful dome a hundred feet above us, and below it a preserved elephant stood majestically, with its head held high.

"Its huge," he whispered.

"Yeah," I said, "elephants are the largest animals on land."

Tay held a museum map in his hands, studying it carefully, uninterested by the massive mammals in front of him.

"Okay, it looks like the diamond's upstairs," he said as he started walking right, walking straight through the doors and never looking up from the map. Taylor and I chased after him, trying not to lose him in the large and increasingly dark museum.

The Hope Diamond was technically part of the hall of gems and minerals, but it had a room all to itself. It sat in a rotating display case all alone in the center of the room, a spotlight from the ceiling shining onto it and reflecting its beauty and grandeur from every possible angle. It really was a beautiful stone, a large, richly colored dark sapphire embedded in a ring of smaller white diamonds and strung on a necklace chain. The walls of the room, however, told me how the last person who had worn it had died, and the person before that, and the person before, and the person before, and the person before, and the—

Bang! Tay slammed his entire backpack into the glass case protecting the diamond. The glass vibrated but didn't break, and he stumbled backwards, dazed.

"What are you doing!?" I yelled, alarmed by his stupidity.

"It won't break!" he snapped.

"Do you really think that's the best way to go about breaking the case?" Taylor asked.

"Well, how about you try it!" Tay retorted, his face reddening. He angrily sat down on the floor, grumbling about *frickin' glass* and *that damned diamond.*

Taylor did try it. He dug his chisel from earlier out of his backpack and slowly tapped away at the glass. I tried to help him, but after twenty minutes we hadn't so much as made a scratch. He finally sank to the floor beside Tay, exhausted and frustrated.

I studied the display case, thinking hard. We couldn't break bulletproof glass with force, as our previous two attempts had proven. Then how *could* we break it? I remembered the lady from my church who could shatter wine glasses with her voice alone, but I didn't think we could make a high enough sound to shatter glass this strong. Heat, maybe? But we'd need something as intense as a flamethrower, maybe something even hotter. I looked at the base of the display case, the area below the glass, and the answer came to me. It was so simple; I couldn't believe we'd missed it.

"Guys!" I shouted. "A keyhole! There should be a key in the curator's office!"

Both boys jumped to their feet it excitement.

"Oh, that's genius! I saw some offices on the way here!" Taylor cried. "Let's go!"

He made a mad dash for the exit, but he stopped dead in his tracks once he got to the doorway. He stood there with his back to us, frozen, not quite in the room but not yet out of it.

"Taylor, what are you waiting for?" I asked.

Then I heard it.

A low growl echoed up the staircase. No, that was two growls, no, it was three creatures growling at once. My heart stopped and all the air left my lungs.

No. Drake told us the werewolves would be gone by now; it wasn't a full moon tonight. It wasn't even totally dark out yet. But something still growled outside the doorway. Slowly, I made my way to where Taylor stood and peeked over his shoulder.

Prowling its way up the staircase was a great, pitch-black, muscular, thick-furred canine the size of a great dane. Its lips were pulled back to reveal a fierce set of pearly white incisors and fangs. It looked right at us, its eyes glowing bright red.

Run, screamed every muscle in my body, *Oh God, you've got to run.*

But there was nowhere *to* run. On the left and right ends of the hallway were two more fierce wolf-monsters, but they were silver and white instead of black, and they were edging their way towards us too. I put my hands on Taylor's shoulders and guided him backwards into the room, never taking my eyes of the fearsome beasts in front of us. Tay stood beside me now, his face pale green. He held three chisels. He gave one to me and one to Taylor with a shaking arm. He grabbed my hand. It was clammy and cold. I took Taylor's hand too. It trembled wildly in mine.

And there we stood, clasping hands, forming an involuntary human barrier in front of the diamond, with chisels as our crude and only weapons as three monster wolves slowly closed in on us. It was the first time on a mission that I had time to wonder if I was going to die.

The three wolves entered the room at the same time, snarling and foaming at their mouths. They stood, glaring at us with their terrible, blood-red eyes. Time stopped. Three wolves. Three humans. It wasn't even a contest. I squeezed Tay and Taylor's hands harder as I waited in fear for something, anything, to happen.

A fierce roar cut through the air as the three wolves pounced, but not on us, on the diamond. We ducked as the one in the middle soared through the air and dove straight into the case, shattering it, and sending fragments of glass, and the diamond, flying. The wolf flailed on its back, trying to get back up again, and I saw our chance for survival.

"RUN!" I screamed as I dashed from the room, pulling Tay and Taylor along with me. Ferocious barks echoed from behind us as two of the dogs gave chase. We sprinted into the gems and minerals exhibit, trying to find an exit in the maze of a museum.

As we ran through the exhibit, the wolves chased after us, slamming into displays and smashing more glass cases with the sheer force of their weight. When I peeked over my shoulder to see how far away they were, I saw that the third one had joined its companions, the Hope Diamond dangling around its neck.

We ran out of the exhibit and into the hall, but we ran too fast. I slammed into the bannister with full force, dragging my friends down with me, knocking sore pain into my bones and the wind out of my lungs.

We scrambled to our feet, still holding hands, and turned right, but this time we weren't fast enough. There was a sudden yanking on my arm as Tay screamed and crashed down to the floor beside me, the white wolf's jaws clenched around his forearm, and the other two wolves close behind.

No! My mind filled with panic, as intense, throbbing pain filled my own arm, but then a second scream drowned out Tay's.

No, not a scream. A scree. In a fuzzy, winged blur Mothman was upon the white wolf, slashing at its neck with his massive claws. The wolf howled in pain and crawled backwards, but Mothman wasn't done. He attacked from the air like a hawk swooping down on a bunny rabbit, grabbing the entire wolf with the talons on his feet and swinging him through the air, sending the beast crashing down upon the elephant in the atrium below.

Mothman turned to the black wolf, the one wearing the diamond, and repeatedly struck his claws across the beast's eyes. This wolf was stronger than its companion, however, and it fought back with ferocious intensity, biting at Mothman's arms. The silver wolf worked to tear into Mothman as well, trying to protect its friend.

Through all the confusion of the moment, Taylor took the lead. He pulled Tay up off the ground and directed him into my arms. "Get him downstairs and out of the museum. I'll get the diamond," he said.

"Taylor, don't!" I tried to call out to him, but it was too late.

He flew above the fighting monsters and tugged the diamond off the wolf's neck, but I could tell he was struggling to stay in the air, his wings flapping overtime as he fought to keep from falling. He looked back and saw me still standing in the same place he left me, holding a dazed and blood-soaked Tay, paralyzed with fear.

"GO!" he yelled.

As he did, the black wolf tried to yank the diamond out of his hand with its mouth, but Taylor wasn't relenting. They were caught in a dangerous game of tug-of-war, and the wolf lost his grip at the wrong moment, the sudden break from the force of his pulling sending the diamond flying from Taylor's grip and over the bannister.

The wolf jumped over the railing after it without hesitation, but part of its body rammed into Taylor, and he lost his balance. He went over the edge of the railing too, but his wings weren't working.

He wasn't flying, he was falling.

I screamed and somehow regained the ability to move. As Mothman ripped his claws into the silver wolf, I held an almost unconscious Tay against me and made a beeline for the staircase. He was leaning on me heavily, his eyes closing, his breathing heavy. Blood poured from the harsh wound on his upper arm.

Don't die, please, don't die. The thought applied to both him and Taylor, who I hoped to God wasn't crumpled and broken on the floor.

It took much longer than it should have, but I burst through the door to the atrium, practically carrying Tay.

"Taylor!" I screamed, frantically scanning the room for any trace of him. The broken corpse of the white wolf lay defeated in a pool of blood. A hot panicked fear rose in my chest at the sight of it, terrified for what the same fall could have done to my friend. "TAYLOR!"

"I'm here!" called a voice from somewhere above me. I looked up, and there was Taylor, on the back of the elephant, no doubt traumatized but otherwise appearing physically sound.

"Ohthankgoodness!" I gasped, relieved of my mini-heart attack, "Can you get down?"

He shook his head and pointed behind and below the elephant. The black wolf snarled up at him from the elephant's back right foot, eyeing something on the elephant's tusk – the diamond! Its string had caught on the tusk, and it now hung suspended it air, too high for the wolf to jump to but too far for Taylor to reach without falling.

A wild howl soared through the air as a red and silver blur came hurtling downwards from the second floor. The wolf crashed into the elephant with such force that its entire head came flying off its body, zooming down the hall with the hope diamond still attached, and the black wolf dashed after it.

In hindsight, I should have just let Tay drop to the floor and run after it too. Mothman probably could have been with me in an instant, and the two of us could have defeated the most likely already injured wolf and wrestled the diamond away from it. But here's where I went wrong; in that moment, I decided the diamond wasn't important anymore. At least, it wasn't nearly as important as keeping Taylor from falling and Tay from bleeding out. And even with two of the wolves dead, I was still terrified to face the black wolf, even with Mothman by my side.

Mothman stood atop the bannister and let out a triumphant "SCRREEEEEEEEEE!!!"

He flew down to the elephant and scooped up Taylor, who climbed on the great moth's back and hung on for dear life as Mothman flew down to me and Tay. He held me in one giant arm and Tay in the other. He scree-ed again, then fluttered upwards towards the broken dome, unable to move too quickly with the added weight of three people.

I looked down and saw something that made my breath catch in my throat. The black wolf sat in the doorway to the hall that the diamond had soared down, and a man dressed in a formal black suit stood beside it, stroking its head as if it were his pet Labrador retriever. He wore the Hope Diamond around his neck, and his face... was only half human. He had pale lips, and a pointed nose, and one green eye. But the left side of his head was that of a black, hairless dog with one pointed ear and a glistening brown eye.

It was him. It was the man who had brought us here, and he was looking right at me. But before I could scream, Mothman soared out of the dome and into the dark, starry sky.

NIGHTMARE

Mothman carried us all the way across the river in a matter of minutes and set us down in a grassy area in Arlington National Cemetery.

"Scraw?" he cooed, eyeing Tay's bloodied arm with concern.

"Oh God," I gasped, seeing the sheer amount of blood that stained his arm and shirt. "Oh, good God." I gingerly took him from Mothman and set him down on the grass. He lay there limply; his eyes open only a sliver. I checked his pulse; it was there, but faint. Taylor whipped off his jacket and I tied it around Tay's arm, making a crude bandage. "I need the—"

I was going to say "first aid kit," but I turned around and realized we had all left our backpacks in the Hope Diamond room at the museum.

"Oh, no no no no no!" I cried. "Taylor, we left our backpacks! I don't have a first aid kit."

Taylor's face lost all its color.

"We can't go back!" he said. "The wolf could still be there."

He was right, but we could go somewhere else.

"Mothman, can you take us to a hospital?" Mothman stared at me blankly, slowing blinking his buggy red eyes.

"Just carry us again. I think I saw one back over the river. I'll tell you when to stop."

Together, Taylor and I lifted Tay and placed him in Mothman's arms. He moaned in pain but didn't open his eyes. We climbed on Mothman's back, and he seemed now to understand what we needed. He rose up into the air, and I pointed to the right.

"There! Go that way!" I said, making sure Mothman could see my hand, and we were off.

We reached the hospital and rushed Tay to an empty bed. I raided the room for the proper supplies and started cleaning and bandaging his wound the best I could. Taylor and I cringed as we the phantom sting of the cleaning agents seeped into our own arms, but it faded quickly enough and was replaced by the sharp throbbing pain we had become used to since Tay was first bitten.

I wrapped a tight bandage around his wound. He still hadn't woken up yet, so all we could do was wait. Taylor pulled the flip phone out of Tay's jeans pocket.

"We... we should probably tell Drake what happened," he said gently.

I swallowed hard. Tay was gravely injured. We had lost our backpacks. We didn't have the diamond, but our enemy did. I wasn't looking forward to explaining this to him.

*****

"Hellhounds," Drake said, after I explained to him what attacked us. "Or maybe dire wolves. Possibly even grims. Either way, my spy trio must have gotten something lost in translation. I'm so sorry. Had I known they weren't werewolves, I would have never sent you after the diamond."

I took a shaky breath in. I didn't blame Drake for the mistake, so I almost said *It's okay*, but it really wasn't. Tay had lost a lot of blood, and Taylor had almost fallen to his death. "Okay" didn't fit the situation at all.

"Mothman was a godsend," Taylor piped up, "He came to the rescue just in time. He really tore up the wolves, and killed two of them." Taylor reached up his arm and scratched under Mothman's chin. Mothman closed his eyes and leaned into Taylor's fingers, purring happily.

"And the third wolf?" Drake asked.

Taylor and I exchanged a nervous glance. "Drake, I'm sorry, but we failed," I said, "The wolf got the diamond. We were literally fighting for our lives," I glanced down at Tay, "They were too strong."

Drake gave a long, deep sigh. "I am disappointed you couldn't secure the diamond," he said, "but I value your lives more."

I was ready to hang up the phone, but there was one more thing I had to tell him.

"Drake..." I began, not sure how to say it. "When we were leaving the museum, I... I s-saw the man with the chupacabra face. The one who brought us here."

The other line went dead silent. Taylor stopped rubbing Mothman's chin and stared at me open mouthed. Mothman let out a curt scree in protest, took Taylor's arm, and moved it back and forth under his chin manually.

"You... what?" Drake said, his voice deathly low.

"He was watching us leave from a hallway, petting the wolf," I explained, "he was wearing the diamond."

"Oh, god," Drake groaned, "oh, that's not good. He was waiting for you. He was waiting to kill you."

It was my turn to be shocked. "What? How?"

"He knows I'm the head of the operation against him, and he's always out to stop me in any way he can. Somehow, he found out I was sending someone after the diamond, and set up a trap." He sighed. "I'm so sorry, children, I— you're in danger. I was going to send you after an object in Virginia, but I need to get you away from here."

Taylor swallowed. "What about tonight? Is he still after us?"

"Oh, you should be safe for the night," Drake said, "it's a big city, and he has no way of tracking you. I'm just fearful he's become aware of my plans for you. I highly suspect he has spies of his own; trios of people he rescues before I can or monsters he trains like I've trained Mothman."

I was relieved that we didn't have to move Tay again, but Drake's description made this man seem powerful, and he frightened me. "I'll text you a new location tomorrow and get to summoning Mothman immediately. He'll bring you new supply bags tomorrow."

"Wait!" I called, sensing that Drake was about to hang up. One question still lingered on my mind.

"Yes, Lori?" Drake asked, his voice feigning patience.

"This man, the one who brought us here... do you know his name?"

Drake paused for a moment, then, "Conan. His name was Conan." He hung up the phone.

I flipped our cellphone shut and held it in my hand for a moment, thinking.

"SCREEEEEEE!!!" Mothman shot out of the room, smelling the juice that Drake had put on a fruit in Area 51. It was just the three of us again. I walked over to Tay's bed and sat on the edge of it. I checked his pulse again. It was stronger than last time; it wasn't quite normal, but it was definitely stronger.

I took his hand in my own and took in a shaky breath, trying as hard as I could not to cry. Taylor sat down beside me and put an arm around my shoulders, tears silently falling down his cheeks. We were in bad shape. We were in really, really bad shape. But we needed to get through this, so I distracted myself the only way I could in this layer. "Taylor," I said gently, my voice barely audible. "I spy, with my little eye, something that is blue."

There was no way we were moving Tay again, so Taylor and I spent the night in the hospital. We wheeled in two rolling beds from the rooms down the hall and placed them next to Tay's. It felt good to lie on an actual mattress for once, and not just under a mess of blankets on the floor, but I couldn't go to sleep just yet. I had to stay up in case something happened to Tay.

As Taylor tried to get some sleep under the too-bright fluorescent hospital lights, I sat cross legged on my bed, watching Tay and thinking. I suppose worrying would be the more accurate term, because I was really just thinking about what would happen if Conan found us. Would he kill us? Kidnap us for torture? There was no way we could fight back, not in the condition we were in now.

I tried to distract myself by thinking of what city Drake might send us to next, but that just reminded me of how Tay had mentioned that he wanted to see Chicago, and that just reminded me of how Tay was unconscious, and that just reminded me of how much he had bled when the wolf bit him, and that just reminded me of how people sometimes die from blood loss, and that just—

No, I needed to stop thinking like that. I looked at the bandage on Tay's arm. He didn't seem to be bleeding through it, but I gently lifted up his arm so I could check the other side. Pain flared up in my own arm, and I quickly put his down again, not wanting to hurt him even in his rest. The bandage was stopping the bleeding on both sides just fine.

Tay let out a faint groan and his eyes slowly blinked open. He tilted his head to look at me.

"Hey," he said faintly.

"Tay!" I cried. Joyous, warm relief flooded my mind. "You're awake!"

"I guess so," he mumbled. He seemed to realize we were in a place he didn't recognize, and he tried to push himself up in bed. A new flash of pain entered my arm, and Tay fell back down onto the mattress, crying out in pain.

"Don't move!" I told him. "That wolf bit you, remember? Just rest. Everything's been taken care of." I sat next to him on the bed now, stroking his hair. He closed his eyes. He said something, but it was so quiet I couldn't understand him.

"Hmm?" I said.

"Did we get the Hope Diamond?" He said, his voice a little louder but still barely audible.

"No," I said gently, "no, we didn't. But it's okay. It's all going to be okay."

He sighed and leaned his head towards me.

"Goodnight, Lori," he said.

"Goodnight, Tay." I replied.

I kept stroking his hair until he fell asleep again. After another hour, his pulse was almost normal, and assuring myself that he was in stable condition, I crawled into my bed and fell asleep too.

I woke up the next morning to the sound of chattering voices.

"... and then, he just left. I know everyone loves Mulder, but it was the worst episode of the first season." I sat up to find Tay and Taylor chatting on one of the beds, and three brand new black backpacks by the door.

"Oh my gosh!" I exclaimed. "You're awake! Mothman was here! Why didn't anyone wake me up?"

"You seemed pretty tired last night," Taylor said, "we thought you could use the rest."

There was no way I was admitting it, but I was grateful. "What time is it?" I asked.

"Noon," Tay said.

"Noon?"

"It's okay," he said, "Drake checked the flight schedule for us, and the next plane to St. Louis doesn't leave for another five hours."

"We're going to St. Louis?"

"Yeah!" Taylor exclaimed. "To one of my favorite places, the City Museum! It's so much fun, I used to go there all the time. But there's a cross there that was used in the Roland Doe exorcism we talked about by those steps yesterday."

I recalled that conversation in my mind, the one about horror movies and all their curses. The thought of an object related to demons made me nervous, but if Taylor knew the museum, we had an advantage.

I stood up and walked over to Tay to examine his arm. It looked healthy enough, but I wasn't going to take any risks. "I'm going to change your bandage," I said, unraveling the gauze on his arm.

"Okay," Taylor said, standing up and grabbing a backpack. "I'll go find a bathroom and get ready for the day."

"Bring us some lunch, too!" Tay called after him. "I'm starving!"

I re-cleaned Tay's wound and put a fresh bandage on it. "It looks good," I told him, "as in, it doesn't look infected or anything." Despite all the pain and blood loss, the wound was unexpectedly shallow. That was good, because I was worried about having to give

Tay stitches, something that I knew how to do in theory, but having never gone to medical school, I'd never actually practiced.

Taylor came back in a fresh jeans and a clean t-shirt from yet another cheap tourist destination, carrying three turkey sandwiches from the hospital cafeteria. "There's a bathroom just down the hall," he said, "it has showers, and the walls are the prettiest shade of mint."

After we ate, we rearranged the supplies in our backpacks, putting the first aid kit in my bag, the maps in Taylor's, and some extra painkillers in Tay's. His arm was still sore, as Taylor and I both knew all too well, but he wasn't losing blood or consciousness anymore, so we walked to a nearby hotel and took one of their shuttle buses to the airport.

We arrived at the airport with three hours until our flight, so we took a souvenir deck of cards from a gift shop and started a game of Liar by the gate. I wasn't very good at it, because Tay was a really good liar and Taylor could always tell when I was lying. We moved on to a game of War, where I found out that Tay had the extraordinary ability of being able to shuffle the cards with incredible speed and precision, and I had the extraordinary ability to always lose no matter how many games we played.

After what seemed like at least a hundred games, we finally boarded the plane. It was a full flight again, and we sat on the ground in the back of the plane, just like we did on our first trip together. So much had changed since then; I had been awkward, fearful, and unbearably shy of everything and everyone in this layer just a few days ago. Now most of that was gone.

Tay leaned against the wall of the plane, trying to sleep, just like he had been during our first flight. I've never been able to sleep on airplanes, but this time something compelled me to join him. I rested my head against his shoulder, like I used to do with Grandma when we would watch movies on the couch on Saturday nights. Tay's muscles tensed for a second, and for a moment I was afraid I was making him uncomfortable, but he relaxed again before I could even open my eyes. Before I knew it, I was out.

I started to dream, but something was off. Usually, when a person starts dreaming, they aren't aware they have had a dream until it's all over and they've woken up. But I knew I was dreaming from the moment the dream started. I stood in a blank landscape, a thick purple and pink fog swirling all around me. It wasn't the kind of thing I usually dreamed about, but it was strangely vivid. I knew it was a dream, but it almost felt like I was awake.

A shadow appeared from the fog in front of me, a person advancing forwards. He emerged from the fog, a man in a fancy black suit, a man with a giant blue diamond around his neck. A man with half a chupacabra's face. Conan.

I stepped backwards, my pulse racing. This was a man who wanted to hurt me. But he spread his arms in a welcoming gesture, as if I had just stepped into his living room for afternoon tea.

"Don't be afraid, Lori," he said, trying to make his voice gentle and inviting. It didn't work. He waved his hand and two plush green arm chairs appeared out of the air and floated to the ground. "Have a seat," he said, "let's have a chat."

I didn't want to sit and "have a chat." I wanted to wake up. I tried to wake up. But I couldn't. Conan waved his arm again and suddenly the chair was behind me, ramming into the backs of my knees until I lost my balance and fell over backwards into it. It zoomed forward to meet his chair, and he sat down across from me. I tried to stand up, to jump to my feet and run away, but again, I couldn't.

"How did you get here?" I croaked.

He chuckled and flicked his wrist. A ghostly copy of the Voynich Manuscript appeared above his palm.

"I do enjoy spellcasting, Lori. Don't you?"

"You-y-you tried to kill me," I stuttered.

Conan shook his head and clicked his tongue. "Lori, Lori, Lori, you really shouldn't believe everything Drake tells you. He's not as smart as he thinks, you know." He waved his arm yet again and a coffee table with a blue porcelain tea set appeared between us. He took a dainty little teacup in his rough and calloused hands, poured himself a glass of steaming tea, and took a sip. "He fell for my trap, after all."

His trap. The wolves *had* been a trap. A wave of rage filled my chest and hot blood pounded in my ears. This man was evil. He was evil, he tried to kill me, and I hated him. "What do you want from me?"

He put down his tea, a condescending expression of mock surprise on his half-human face. "What do I want from you?" he mimicked. "I think you should be asking about what you can get from me."

"I don't want anything from you," I said.

"Oh?" he asked. "Are you sure? Because a little birdie told me somebody's Grandma just died."

My blood froze. How did he know that? He leaned in closer to me. "And *this* little birdie would like to tell you that there are methods of getting her back."

Getting her back? Did he mean... raising my Grandma from the dead? As much as I missed her, I knew I couldn't live with a zombie. That was unnatural, and it went against her religion.

"I — I couldn't." I stammered.

"Mm, I think you could. All you have to do is help me."

"I would never!"

"Don't be snappy, this will benefit you too. You'll steal artifacts for me instead of Drake. And when we reach the layer of the Unreal, I'll help you find Grandma, you'll help me find my brother and fiancée, we'll go our separate ways and live out nice, new lives in our nice new layer with our dear old friends. Sounds pleasant, doesn't it?"

I swallowed, hard. That wouldn't be bringing Grandma back from the dead, not really. It meant instead that I would live with her in a strange new world, and not live with my cousin. I wouldn't have to go to Providence or public school. I could be with Grandma again, and I knew that no matter what happened, everything else would be okay as long as I had her by my side. I stopped myself from getting too deep into the happy thought. There were other consequences to consider.

"What about Tay and Taylor?" I asked.

Conan shrugged. "I would just tell you to run away, but you can't get farther than a mile or so from your trio, can you? We'll just... dispose of them. Like Drake did to his companions. Unless they want to help me too. I'm sure they have someone they'd like to find in the Unreal, too."

But he was wrong. Tay and Taylor had no family and few friends and their parents, even if they weren't still alive, didn't want them. They had no reason to betray Drake, and I couldn't betray them. I couldn't let Conan kill them, if that was what he was hinting at, not after everything we'd been through. I shut my eyes tight and forced my love for my grandma out of my mind. I couldn't let everyone else in this layer suffer for my gain. Besides, what proof did Conan have that his plan wouldn't kill us? What proof did he have that his family would even want him anymore, after what he'd become? Could Grandma ever love me again after all the blood that would inevitably get on my hands from trying to find her? No, she couldn't. And I wouldn't be able to live with myself, either.

"I'm not helping you," I said, matter-of-factly.

Conan's face hardened, his cruel smile gone. "I thought you would be the sensible one," he said, "I thought you, of all people, would understand where I'm coming from. I thought you'd need to see your Grandma to be happy."

"I'm not happy without her, but I can't go looking for her. She'd want me to move on." I looked in his eyes now, the canine iris brown, the human one green. "Maybe you should, too."

A fire raged in Conan's pupils and he rocketed from his chair in fury. "Your grandma lived a full life, my family was taken from me unfairly! They never got to live like they wanted to and I haven't either!" His face was right in mine, his mouth snarling. After a moment, he gave a deep exhale and sank back into his chair. "I was wrong about you. You didn't love her like I loved them." And with that, I woke up.

I bolted upright, scaring the living daylights out of the unprepared Tay beside me.

"Jesus, Lori!" He cried, which got Taylor's attention too. "What is up with you?"

I knew I should explain to them what had happened, that I saw Conan and that he tried to make a deal with me. But the dream also felt so personal, the way Conan had talked about my Grandma and of "disposing of" Tay and Taylor. It was the kind of thing I wanted to keep to myself. I felt like I needed to think about the dream some more before I spoke, but with my friends staring at me, I had to say something.

"I... I had a nightmare." They held their gaze, sensing that something was wrong. Tay cleared his throat. "You had a nightmare and...?"

"The man who brought us here, Conan, he came to me. He tried to get me to help him. I turned him down."

My friends' eyes were open wide, their faces shocked.

"Wait," Tay said, "he came to you? You saw him?"

"Are you sure it was him? Are you sure he wasn't just in your head?" Taylor asked.

"Yes," I said, "well, no. I mean, yes. Well..." I took a deep breath. "The dream felt very real. It was very clear, and I usually don't dream like that. I tried to wake up, but I couldn't until the conversation was over. And it was definitely him. He had the face and the diamond."

There was another uncomfortable moment of silence as Tay and Taylor tried to comprehend what I was saying.

"You need to tell this to Drake," Taylor said.

"No!" I said, with more force than I meant to. "I mean; I want to wait at least until we land. I need to think about it more. It scared me."

There was nothing else they could make me do. Tay sighed and leaned back against the wall. "Alright, whatever." Taylor reluctantly went back to his doodles on a napkin. I was left alone to my thoughts.

I hadn't registered it before, but Taylor's mention of Drake brought something else Conan had said to the forefront of my thoughts. *We'll just... dispose of them. Like Drake did to his companions.* What did he mean by that? The Drake I knew seemed incapable of harming anyone; he was nerdy, even awkward, gentle with Mothman and everyone else. Perhaps Conan had just thrown a lie into his speech to scare me, or to convince me that killing your trio is common and somehow not immoral in the slightest. But the words didn't seem deliberate; the more I repeated them in my head, the more they sounded like a footnote or an afterthought, something you throw into a conversation at the last second because you've just remembered it's relevant. Conan didn't say those words for their shock factor, because if he was using them for that purpose he would have gone into more detail. He would have used the sentence as further evidence as to why I shouldn't trust Drake. It was almost like Conan thought he was mentioning something I already knew.

The more I thought about what Conan had said, the more mysterious Drake seemed to me. How much did I know about him really? I knew his name, what he looked like, where he worked, but what had his life been like before I'd known him? Could I really trust him anymore?

I pushed the thoughts aside. I was letting Conan mess with my head. Maybe Drake had been a murderer. Maybe he hadn't. I could interrogate him later, grab my trio and run far away if I needed to, but for now I didn't have any choice but to believe he was on my side. He had saved me from the desert, given me a backpack full of survival gear, and offered me a safe place to stay if the world outside became too scary. I had no way of telling what he had done in the past, but in the present, I really believed Drake was doing his best to help me.

I ran over the dream in my mind for the rest of the flight, struggling to convince myself that yes, it really was real, and yes, it really was Conan talking to me. It was too deliberate to have been something my subconscious had made up. I didn't fully understand how he could come to me in dreams, but somehow, using some odd words from the Voynich Manuscript, he could.

The part about him asking for my help and the threats on my friends' lives and the insults of Drake all upset me, but the last thing Conan had said was what my mind kept coming back to. He said that I didn't love my Grandma like he loved his family. That because he couldn't let them stay dead, they meant more to him than she did to me. The claim made me angry because I knew he wasn't just saying it to make me upset; his face showed that he truly believed his words. He was wrong, but he'd never see things my way. I was making my Grandma proud by continuing my life and by trying to become a nurse like her: I was carrying on her legacy. I knew she wouldn't want me to bring her back from the dead or search for her spirit. I was showing my love for her exactly how she would have wanted me to, and my love for her was both incomprehensible and infinite, no matter what Conan said.

EXORCIST

After a few more grueling hours of flying in uncomfortable silence, we landed in the St. Louis airport, the sky already dark. We stopped for dinner at a little burger place in the terminal. We took our food from the kitchen and ate in silence, one thing on everybody's mind.

"So, Lori..." Taylor began. "Are you ready to call Drake yet?"

"I don't want to talk about it," I snapped. "I'll call him when I'm ready."

We ate the rest of our meal without anyone uttering another word.

We walked out to the cabs parked outside the airport and hopped in a shuttle to a nice hotel downtown. Taylor longingly gazed out the window at the darkened city the whole time. I remembered suddenly that this was his hometown, the place that he'd been before he was pulled into this layer.

"Is it weird to be back?" I asked him.

"Kinda," he said, "it feels a little alien. I know I'm here, but the city doesn't." He was right. Nowhere felt quite the same from this layer.

"Did you live around here?" I said.

"No, we were more to the west," he replied.

I remembered the vision I had seen, of him and another girl playing around giant turtle statues. That family didn't seem like they planned on returning to a house filled with countless other orphans and a pet parrot. My curiosity got the best of me and I tried my luck and see how much Taylor was willing to reveal about his past.

I coughed. "Did you always live in the same house, or…"

His face dropped, and I instantly felt guilty for prying. "I lived with an actual family once. I had two foster parents and their daughter was my best friend. But... I have some learning disabilities. I got overwhelmed by school and a lot of other things. They couldn't handle that. I was put in a home for kids who were more like me."

From the day we first met, I had always known Taylor's mind was different, but I never thought he was different in a bad way. He was quirky and a little weird sometimes, but I never knew that would be enough to tear him away from a family, from a chance at being loved. I wasn't sure what to say, but I felt terrible for making him relive a memory he was obviously still hurting from.

I felt the need to apologize, but he turned away from me and continued staring at the city lights. I cleared my throat. "Taylor, I—"

He touched my arm, eyes still stuck to the window glass, and pointed. "Look, there's the arch!" The big silver loop was much taller than I had expected, and it was beautifully lit up against the dark night sky.

"Wow," I whispered. We didn't have such famous architecture in Concord, New Hampshire.

"And there's the old capital building," he continued, pointing to a domed structure just below the arch. "And there's Park East Tower. And there's the Civil Courts Building. And there's the..."

He pointed out place after place to me, naming parks and skyscrapers and schools and statues as we passed them by. I wondered how he could keep track of so many places; his memory must have been incredible.

We arrived at the hotel, (which Taylor had pointed out to me as the hotel before we arrived) pulled our backpacks off the bus, and followed one of the other passengers to his room. We arranged our faux-beds on the floor and got ready to settle in for the night, but it was only eight o'clock. It was too late to go to the City Museum, but too early to actually go to sleep. The man in the real layer lay in bed with a book, keeping the lights on.

"Well," Tay said, glancing at the clock. He took the TV remote off the bedside table. "You guys want to watch something?"

I didn't really watch TV all that often at home, but there wasn't much else to do in the hotel room. Tay clicked the power button on the remote, and the television flickered to life, a news broadcast on the screen.

"That's right, Jim, there was no sign of forced entry, no damage done to the exhibit, and a security camera malfunction picked up nothing," said the anchor. There was an image of a big, blue gemstone on the screen. The Hope Diamond. They were talking about us – about our attempted theft.

"Oh, Christ," Tay mumbled.

"It's alright," Taylor said, "it's just like Drake told us. They think it was a robbery, a perfectly executed robbery."

"Can we change it?" I said, "I know they don't know that was our fault, but it still makes me nervous."

Tay picked up the remote and changed the channel. It was an ad for an insurance company. He changed it again, and ironically, *The Exorcist* was on. Tay laughed. "Would you look at that?" he said. I didn't think it was very funny. Seeing the displeasure on my face, he flipped the channel yet another time. More ads. "Ugh," he grumbled, "what do you guys usually watch?"

"Not much," I said, "I'm not that into TV."

"I actually like the commercials," Taylor remarked. Tay groaned. "Well, you guys are no help."

He changed the channel one more time, to a documentary on sharks. He smiled. "Oh, I love these," he said, "does anybody mind?"

"Works great for me," Taylor said, already mesmerized by the footage of the giant fish in the vast blue ocean.

"As long as they don't show it attacking anybody..." I said. Just because I wanted to be a nurse didn't mean I liked seeing people get hurt.

"They won't," Tay assured me. "See, it doesn't have any teeth, it's a basking shark. It eats plankton."

To my relief, it turned out that the documentary showcased harmless sharks, and Tay gave us extra facts every time they showed a new species.

"You'd never guess by looking at it, but that's called a zebra shark."

"That one there is the third biggest shark in the ocean."

"Oh! Look Lori, a *nurse* shark!"

"You really know your sharks," I told him. His knowledge surprised me, this wasn't the type of thing I'd expect him to be into.

"Oh, yeah," he said, "There's an aquarium on Pier 41 that my old foster parents had membership to. They'd take all us kids there every weekend." He sighed contently, remembering. "There're a ton of sharks living in the bay, too. I used to sit on the piers and look for leopard sharks. I still do, sometimes."

I couldn't quite tell why, but Tay's shark-filled memories made me happy. "That sounds like fun," I said. "The only animals we see in Concord are robins and squirrels."

We finished up the documentary just as the person in the real layer flipped off the lights. The credits rolled over footage of a nurse shark swimming away from the camera and into the vast, blue ocean.

Tay sighed contentedly, his eyes full of love for his favorite types of fish. "Well," he said, "you guys ready to go to bed now?" No sooner did the question escape his lips than did the ground start to shake.

"Earthquake!" I cried, balling into the armadillo hands-over-your-neck position they had taught us in elementary school. Tay and Taylor, in a panic and having no ideas of their own, joined me. The shaking stopped after a few seconds, and I slowly lifted up my head and had a look around. Nothing was out of place at all – the pictures hung neatly on the walls, the furniture was right where we left it, and the person in the real layer still lie in bed, undisturbed.

"This earthquake must have just been in our layer," I said to Tay and Taylor, pointing to the sleeping real layer man.

"But why would there be an earthquake in our layer?" Taylor asked. "Unless it was some kind of mystical, make-believe earthquake?" He had a point, there was no reason for a belief in earthquakes to be disputable enough to put one into an unreal layer.

I wandered over to the window to check on the world outside and make sure it really had been just in our layer. All the buildings seemed normal, like they hadn't been moved, but the world outside had changed in a different way. I could see unreal beings in the streets, much more than the occasional monster or ghost we had seen before. Now there seemed to be something mystical on every block; a fairy in the office building next to us, a ghost roaming the sidewalk, a monster hiding in a tree. Tay stared at the wonders out the window beside me, and Taylor peered at them from over my shoulder.

"Those weren't there before, were they?" Tay asked slowly.

Taylor shook his head. "They most definitely were not."

The phone in Tay's pocket started to ring, and he picked it up and put it on speakerphone. "Drake, something strange just happened—"

"We've changed layers," Drake interrupted, "Conan harnessed the power of some special objects and sent us farther from the real layer. We all felt it."

The three of us looked to each other in confusion. "Would you mind explaining that some more?" Taylor asked.

Drake took a deep breath and started again, "This layer still has all the buildings and objects are in our real layer, just like our previous layer did. But in moving us back a layer, Conan had taken everyone in the previous layer back from reality a level. We are now living amongst beings from this layer and beings from the previous layer. There are more beings in this layer because it is farther from reality, and the farther from reality the layer, the more mind-created beings have accumulated within it. To summarize, your surroundings will not appear to have changed, the beings surrounding you have increased, and it will take extra power from universal object to get us home. Understand?"

I did, but the explanation wasn't pleasant. The idea of extra supernatural creatures surrounding us at all times scared me. But more than that, I was further from home instead of closer to it. It made me feel like stealing Annabelle and Mercy's skull had been all for naught.

"Did Conan harness the power of the Hope Diamond for this?" I asked.

"It's a very powerful object," Drake confessed, "I'm afraid so." Great, not only was I feeling frustrated and scared, but guilty, too.

"Thank you, Drake," I said. I snapped the phone closed in Tay's hand, cutting the conversation short.

Tay sunk unto the edge of the bed, his head in his hands. "Great," he said, "so this whole thing is our fault. That's just freakin' awesome. Spectacular."

"Don't remind me," I mumbled.

"Now what?" Taylor asked.

"We get the cross like we planned. He said our environment's still the same." I snapped. I didn't want to talk anymore. I was feeling a lot of things, but none of them were positive. I crawled under my blankets without saying another word, and the other two eventually followed, not wanting to test me. Smart of them.

As I lie awake thinking, a new emotion flooded me, something I hadn't felt in a long, long, time.

Rage. Pure, hot red boiling rage against Conan, for all he had done to me. My anger filled me with determination. I was going to bring him down.

I woke up the next morning feeling more exhausted than I had been when I went to sleep. I trudged to the bathroom and threw on fresh clothes, feeling the emotional turmoil from yesterday all over again. Between the shift in layers and losing the Hope Diamond, I was feeling like we couldn't catch a break.

Tay took his turn in the bathroom next, and I joined Taylor at the window, where he was snapping pictures of the strange beasts in the world below. I knew he was just doing it because they fascinated him, but it wasn't a bad idea for some training. If we could figure out what roamed this new layer, we could figure out how to fight it. We wouldn't be caught off guard again.

"Can I see your pictures?" I asked Taylor.

"Of course!" he said, clicking through the camera's memory screen, excited to share what he had seen. With each photo he commented on something about appearance – the pretty sparkling pattern of some fairy creatures, the detail of the scales of a lizard-type monster, the hombre coloration of a ghost.

"That's all very nice," I told him. "But how many of these pictures have a monster in them that we can name?" We flipped through each photo again, identifying what little we could. I grabbed a pad of paper and pen from the desk in the room and wrote down the names – fairy, ghost, sea serpent. I took the smart phone of the still asleep man in the real layer and tried Googling the rest – "pale lizard man," "flying horned goat," "fiery skeletal shadow" – and I was able to get a few more things identified, but not everything.

"I'm going to research them more whenever we have some downtime," I told Taylor. "If we know what we're up against, we can fight it."

He nodded, contemplating my plans. "You could send some pictures to Drake, too. Remember his office? It was full of all those books and papers. I'm sure he can tell us anything."

"Good idea," I said, and I really meant it. Despite what Conan claimed, Drake was an expert on this kind of stuff.

Tay emerged from the bathroom and Taylor went to take his turn. I told him my plans and showed him the list and photos. I could see a sort of sparking fire behind his eyes when I mentioned I was doing this so we could fight. *So he feels the rage, too*, I thought, *He won't stand to be a victim either*. He helped me name some more of the creatures Taylor and I had missed until Taylor finished getting ready. Together, we marched downstairs, with new plans and a renewed sense of vengeance.

We trekked down the sidewalk en route to the City Museum, following Taylor because he knew the way by heart.

"You guys are going to love it!" he exclaimed as we dodged the ghost of a woman in a blue nightgown running down the street and sobbing. "It's not really a museum," he continued amiably, "well, it sort of is. There are some museum-like exhibits, like the doorknob collection, but it's really more like an indoor and outdoor interactive art piece-slash-playground-slash-maze. They really just called it a museum because there isn't a word for what it is." I looked at Tay, hoping he was as confused as I was. How where we supposed to find one measly cross in a place like that?

We arrived at the museum building, and it looked normal enough. I mean, it didn't look like a museum, but it seemed like your average city building. Taylor told us that it used to be a shoe factory, and the tall, yellowish limestone building looked like it could still serve that purpose. That is, until you looked up and saw the giant praying mantis and the school bus hanging off the roof. Taylor followed my gaze to the top of the building. "Oh, the roof! I forgot about the roof!" he said, "The roof is fun."

Taylor pulled open the door and ushered us inside to the ticket booth, which, because we couldn't physically buy any tickets if we tried, we promptly walked around. The museum was closed today, anyway, which was good, because otherwise we would have had to wait until nightfall so that people wouldn't be around to witness a haunted cross floating in midair.

After we passed through the lobby, we entered a wide room with thousands of long, silver fiberglass stalagmites lining the ceiling. Mosaicked pillars dotted the room, along with a giant white whale, a pterodactyl hanging from wires in the air, an oversized slinky shaped tube leading into the ceiling, a koi pond, and what seemed to be an indoor overgrown jungle in the area to our far right, along with countless other statues and oversized knick-knacks.

All I could say was, "Wow." The place was cluttered, but cluttered in a way that begged you to explore it. All the junk within the room was weird, yet magnificent and wondrous in its own right. We had only been in one room and I could already see why Taylor loved the place so much: it was a hub of crazy, wonderful, colorful, childlike creativity.

Taylor turned to us, smiling as he watched me and Tay react with fascination and curiosity to the strange place before us. "Come on!" he said. "Just wait till you see the rest of it!

We passed into the area to our left and peered through the windows at the fenced-in backyard. It was the jungle gym of every kid's (and, to be honest, adult's) dreams. Colorful chicken wire and slinky-metal tunnels connected giant slides, castle towers, and even airplanes among other wonders, creating a humongous, crazy maze suspended in air. It looked like the kind of place that was too dangerous for human use, but it sure looked like fun.

Taylor led us up a rainbow, paint-splattered staircase to the third floor. We followed him into a room filled with concrete skate park ramps. "They use those as slides," he remarked. He paused for a moment, scanning the walls of the room, thinking. Tay put a hand on his shoulder.

"Dude, this place is awesome. It's beyond awesome," he said, "but where's the cross?"

"That's what I'm trying to remember," Taylor said, "I haven't been here in a while, and it's not really the star attraction, as you could probably tell by now. Most people come here to crawl through the tunnels and use the slides. There's a place with walls full of flashy stuff in the next room, and an architecture exhibit after that. I don't remember seeing any crosses in there, but I think that's where it would probably be."

I exchanged a glance with Tay. He shrugged.

"That makes sense to me," I said, "lead the way."

Taylor took us through a neon barrage of junk that was 50s nostalgia combined with a sketchy circus side show, complete with arcade machines, electric guitars, and two dead rats on the wall. We searched for anything that even remotely resembled a cross, but we didn't find it. Part of me worried that it was still hidden amongst the absurdly large mess of junk, but the other part of me was anxious to leave the eerie exhibit, so I let Taylor lead us into the architecture room.

The gallery more resembled a traditional, non-cluttered museum exhibit, but it still lacked any display cards or information on the walls. It was a beautiful space; filled with ornate columns, gargoyles, archways, and other concrete and stone decor. Unfortunately, there were no crosses among the facades. We left the exhibit, Taylor nervously chewing his lip. "I just don't know where else it could be," he said.

"Don't worry, we've got time," I reminded him. "It's still early. We can search the whole museum if we need to."

He sighed and walked over to the bannister of the rainbow staircase, looking down at the other floors below. "We could, but this place is a huge maze. People get lost in here all the time. There's no way we can find every nook and cranny."

Tay tapped him on the shoulder. "Is that it?" he asked, pointing to the wall behind us. Taylor and I turned around to see a massive, four-foot-long rusted metal cross perched on the wall.

Taylor's eyes widened. "Yes!" he cried. "Yes! That's it!"

Sure enough, a little display card (so this museum *did* use them after all) explained that this cross once sat atop the Alexian Brothers' Hospital, the place where the exorcism of Roland Doe commenced so many years ago.

"Wow, that's huge," Tay remarked, "I was expecting something you could carry in one hand." We were definitely going to need more than just one hand to get this thing out the door. It was bigger than my torso.

Tay stood on the tips of his toes, reached up the wall, and tugged on the cross, trying to separate its base from the screws that held it to the wall.

"Careful, Tay, it'll fall on you!" I admonished. I shooed him over to one side and took hold of the other. We tried wriggling the cross away from the wall, but it wasn't budging.

Tay bit his lip. "Alright, looks like we're going to have to pull harder. Taylor, stand back. On the count of three," he said. "One, two, THREE!"

I used all my weight to try and force the cross off the wall, but it didn't move an inch.

"What the hell?" Tay cried. "That should have worked!" He stood on his tiptoes to try and peer behind the object. "What kind of supports are they using?" He poked his head behind the cross and jerked it back with a yelp, covering his nose with his hands.

A tiny black demon-creature popped out from behind the cross to swat at Tay again. It was smaller than a guinea pig, with big, foxlike ears and leathery black wings. It had the stereotypical pointed devil tail and little goat horns too. It muttered curses in a strange language, speaking in a high-pitched squeak of a voice like something out of a Looney Tune. Tay took his hand off his nose to reveal three itty-bitty scratches.

"It clawed me!" he cried. "It clawed me like a cat!" The critter laughed, stuck out its tongue, and ducked back into its hiding spot behind the cross.

"I think that's why we couldn't move it," I said, "he doesn't want to let it go."

"Yes, but what the heck was it?" Tay asked angrily, glaring at the cross.

"It kind of looked like a demon," Taylor said, "maybe the one that possessed Roland. Maybe's that's why he hangs out around the cross."

Tay groaned. "Lori, how do we get rid of demons? You read anything about that?"

"No," I said, "but I have an idea. Whatever it is, it's not very big. We can just shoo it away with a stick or something, then grab the cross and go."

"That sounds easy enough," Taylor said. "Let's give it a try." He put down his backpack and fished out his flashlight. "I'll get him out with this," he said. I appreciated his positive attitude and open mind as opposed to Tay's grumbling and scowled face, but then again, only one of the two had just had a set of claws swiped across his nose.

Tay and I stood in front of the cross while Taylor approached from the side. "Hey, little guy," he cooed, "we're just gonna move ya reeeeal... quick!" He jabbed the flashlight behind the cross on the last word, sending the little demon flying out the other side. The creature squealed and moaned, flailing on its back in confusion. It flew up to Taylor's flashlight, trying to push it away, but Taylor gave the critter a gentle bop on the head for every time it tried in vain to grab hold of it.

Tay and I looked at each other. *Now*, he mouthed. We gave a mighty tug and the cross came right off the wall, causing us to almost drop it in surprise; it was much heavier than I was expecting. We shifted our grips so that we each held an arm of the cross, and we raced towards the stairs. A tiny, infuriated squeal sounded from behind us, along with Taylor calling, "No no no, come back!"

The cross suddenly weighed less than a feather and I began to feel it rising right out of my hands. The little demon had landed on the cross and was pulling it away from us with the strength of ten men. Tay and I watched helplessly as the demon yanked the cross away and carried it back to where it had been hanging, wrapping its arms around it and scooting back into the wall, rebuilding its hiding spot and making the cross seem as if it had never been moved at all. It all happened in less than a minute.

Taylor poked at the little demon with his flashlight a few more times, but this time it wouldn't budge. We tried tugging the cross off the wall again, but that wasn't moving either. "Wow, he's strong," remarked Taylor, booping it on the head again. "Aren'tcha?"

Tay groaned and ran his fingers through his hair. "Alright, how do we get the cross now?" We all thought about that for a moment. The demon was small and mostly helpless, and even though we definitely could, I didn't want to kill it. We could probably catch it off guard and push it away from the cross again, but it would steal its hiding place back soon enough, unless...

"We could trap it," I quipped. My companions stared at me, waiting for an explanation. "We push it out, then put a box on top of it," I said, "or we get it into another room and shut the door."

"That could work, but that thing's pretty strong," Tay said, "We won't be able to keep it trapped for long."

"Okay, we just trap it long enough to hide the cross outside the museum and for Mothman to get here. He's fast enough that he'll get it away from here before the demon can find it again."

"Wow," Taylor said, "sounds like a plan!"

"Yeah," Tay agreed, "let's go find a trap."

After summoning Mothman with the spray and an apple, Taylor lead us back into the exhibit of clutter, where we searched for anything strong enough to contain an angry demon-critter. He and Tay saw a square, box-like shelf that they thought could work, but it was several feet off the wall, out of reach. Tay was trying to hold Taylor steady as he tried to pull it from the wall while using his wings to hover in mid-air. I could tell that was going to take a while, so I walked a little bit away to search on my own.

Something I hadn't noticed before caught my eye: a little model train village. Well, it was more of a tiny city than a village; complete with office buildings, a factory, and a brownish-red river. Some sort of wire dome sat over one of the buildings, and I wondered if we could use that to trap the demon instead. I started towards the table, but the sound of a train whistle stopped me in my tracks.

No, it stopped me over a set of tracks. Train tracks. A three-foot tall conductor car was speeding towards me, and I scrambled out of the way. Behind it, the other train cars carried a single-file row of chairs; it was a children's ride. But there was no one in the train, how was it running? I was sure it hadn't been when I had first been back here.

The train rumbled towards a tunnel in the wall, and the whistle blared yet again. A curt yelp echoed from the tunnel, and an animal darted out of the way. *Oh great, what am I going to have to fight now?* The creature seemed small enough, I walked towards it only to discover that it was shaped like something I recognized. A long tail, pointy ears, four paws, big green eyes; it was a cat! It was hairless, which explained why I hadn't recognized it sooner, and it was a little beat up, with chunks of its ears missing and clusters of blue veins showing through its skin, but it was a cat nonetheless. And I *loved* cats. Grandma had owned a big, long haired tortoiseshell named Duchess we had until I was ten. Duchess was the sweetest kitty in the world, and she was my best friend for years. She would run to the door to greet me every day when I came home from school, and she would sleep at the foot of my bed every night. Until Grandma's passing, Duchess's death was the saddest I'd ever been in my life. Remembering my dear Duchess and my fondness of cats in general, I got over my shock and slowly advanced towards the creature.

"Here, kitty kitty!" I cooed. The cat looked up.

"Mrrrrrooooow," it said. I didn't know what that meant, but I said "Good kitty!" anyway. I bent down beside the cat and held out my hand for it to sniff. It did for a few moments, and then pushed its head under my palm, begging for affection. I patted the cat's head and ran my hand down its back. It was so skinny; I could feel its spine. I picked the cat up, and it purred in my arms. It didn't look so scary to me anymore, but it sure didn't look cute, either. It just looked kind of...

"Spooky," a small voice said. I turned around in a startled panic. A small, pale girl stood in the entrance to the train tunnel. She had plain, long, pale hair, and an even plainer, paler pink dress on. She flinched when we made eye contact and retreated into the tunnel a bit. Then, she regained her nerve and took a small step forward. "That's what I call him," she said. She stepped completely out of the tunnel now, and I realized that I could see right through her. She was a ghost.

We stared at each other in silence for a bit, because my shyness was coming back because the little girl was a ghost and I was not expecting to meet a ghost and what do you even say to a ghost and oh, no, I was holding her cat and she was probably worried I was stealing it and-

Her cheeks turned pink and she turned away to dash back into the tunnel. "Wait!" I cried. She turned back to me. *Shoot, what now?* I still didn't know what to say to her, but I didn't want her to leave.

"Uhhh," I stammered, struggling to find something to say. "Is this your cat?"

She came out of the tunnel a little more. "Not really," she said, "he lives here, and I play with him a lot, but he takes care of himself. He's not really anyone's cat."

"Oh," I said, running a hand over the purring kitty in my arms. "He's a good cat."

"Yes," she said, "I like him very much."

She tiptoed all the way out of the tunnel now, but still hovered near the entrance. "My name is Winnie," she offered. "It's short for Winona."

"My name is Lori," I told her. "It's short for Taylor."

"We've been watching you," she said, inching forward. "The museum wasn't supposed to be open today. When we realized that you were in our layer, we thought you wanted to hurt us. So we've all been hiding. But your friend was gentle with Charlie, and you're nice to Spooky. I know you aren't going to hurt us now."

"N-no, I'd never hurt you!" I stammered. "All we want is the cross. We need it to get home." I paused for a moment, considering the other things she'd said (who was *we*?), carefully choosing what questions were the most important in helping me get the cross. "Who's Charlie?" I decided to ask.

"He's the imp."

"The imp?"

"The one behind the cross."

"Oh, so that's what it's called."

"Yeah. Imps are like tiny demons, but more mischievous. He's not going to let you take his cross very easily." I definitely agreed with her.

"Winnie, we really need that cross," I said, "we were going to trap him to try and hold him off, but we don't know if that'll work. Can you help us?"

She thought about that for a moment. "What do you need it for?"

I hoped she'd understand the truth, because that was what I decided to tell her. "We aren't from this layer originally, we're from the real layer. A careless man pulled us here by mistake, and a scientist can use objects like the cross to send us back. But if the careless man gets the cross, we'll get pulled even farther from home."

"Did the man have a strange face? Half of it was a dog's?" she asked.

"Y-yeah," I said. *How does she know him?* "Have you seen him?"

"He came here a while ago, but he wasn't looking for the cross. He wanted something else, but he couldn't find it. I hid the whole time he was here. He wasn't good like you," she explained.

My blood turned cold at the thought of Conan having roamed these very halls.

"We know what he's doing," she said, "he's going to move everyone far away. We don't want to go." She stood beside me now and reached up to pet Spooky, who still purred in my arms. "I can help you," she said.

The chill in my blood was replaced by the warm feeling of gratitude in my heart. Winnie trusted me. She thought I was good, and she wanted to help.

A loud crash echoed from the other room, followed by Tay and Taylor cheering. "I think they found a box to trap Charlie." I said.

"I can hold him while he's in there," she said, "I can touch him, but he can't touch me. His claws go right through me. I don't have flesh anymore."

"Are you sure you'll be strong enough, Winnie?" I asked. "Charlie pulled that heavy cross right out of my hands."

"Oh yes, I'm plenty strong enough," she insisted, puffing her chest. "I hold him all the time. I like to hold all the little animals here. He doesn't like it very much, though."

"Lori! Lor-i!" I could hear Tay calling my name from the next room, searching for me. Winnie's face looked panicked and she started to fade away.

"Wait! I thought you wanted to help me!" I cried.

"I will," she said, "I'll be invisible, but I'll hold Charlie in his box."

"You don't want to meet my friends?" I asked.

She shook her head no. "They aren't meant to see me like you are. But I'll be watching. I promise I'll be ready," she said. And with that, she faded away into thin air.

Tay and Taylor just then came around the corner, carrying a big wooden box. "Hey Lori, we — whoa!" Tay yelped, pointing at me with a sudden fear in his voice. "What *is* that!?" I looked down at Spooky, who was now asleep. I had forgotten I was still holding him.

"Oh," I said, "he's a hairless cat. His name is Spooky." I set him down, and he woke up and meowed in protest, causing Tay to jump back.

"That is not a *cat*."

"Yes, he is," I corrected.

"Cats have fur. Cats are cute. That's not a cat."

"You'll hurt his feelings," I said. I relented to Spooky's begging and scratched behind his misshapen ears.

"Where did he come from, Lori?" Taylor asked, coming over to me to examine Spooky.

"He ran out of the tunnel when the train came by. He lives here," I said, leaving out the part about Winnie on purpose. If she didn't want to meet my friends, I doubted she'd want me to tell them about her.

"Well, we got the box. Let's go get the cross," Tay said, anxiously eyeing Spooky as he walked towards the architecture hall.

"Bye, Spooky," Taylor said, standing up to follow him.

I patted the kitty on the head one last time before putting him down and starting to walk away. Spooky yowled in protest, jumped up, and followed me, jogging beside my feet into the next room. Tay was giving the box to Taylor when he turned around and saw us. "What is it doing here?" he asked, letting go of the box too soon so that Taylor almost dropped it.

"He followed me," I said.

"Well, get it out of here!" he cried.

"He's not hurting anyone, Tay," Taylor said.

A twitch came over Tay's face as he scowled at the cat.

"Fine," he said, "but don't let it touch me."

Tay took the flashlight from his bag and stood on the left side of the cross while I stood on the right. Taylor stood to the far right with the box raised, ready to trap Charlie the Imp as soon as Tay shoved him out. Tay peeked behind the cross.

"I think he's asleep now," he remarked. "Perfect." I looked over my shoulder and saw a very faint Winnie waiting behind us. She gave me a shy smile, and I smiled back. Tay pulled back his flashlight.

"Okay," he said, "everybody get ready. One, two, three!"

He rammed the flashlight into the imp and sent him soaring through the air. He landed a good fifteen feet away, where Taylor jumped on him with the box and threw his body on top of it, holding it down with all his weight as Charlie screamed and shook the crate with fury. I could see the faint outline of Winnie, too, her arms going through both the box and Taylor to pin the Imp to the floor.

Tay and I yanked the cross away from the wall and ran.

"The slide!" Taylor called, pointing to a giant slide encased in a ribcage of metal wires. "Send it down the slide!"

Tay laid down at the mouth of the slide and I set the cross down on top of him. He wrapped his arms around it like a mummy holding a jewel and slid down three stories in a matter of seconds. I was about to join him when I heard a loud "SCREEEEEEEEEEE!!" I couldn't see him yet, but Mothman was somewhere outside the museum.

I dashed back to Taylor, grabbed his backpack, and snatched the apple. I ran back to the slide and rolled it down to Tay. "Get it to Mothman as fast as you can!" I cried. He picked up the apple and hobbled outside as quickly as he could while carrying a four-foot-long tin cross and a piece of fruit. I ran back to Taylor, who was struggling to keep Charlie under control, even with Winnie's help. I grabbed a corner of the box and tried to hold it in place as it shook wildly from Charlie's attempts at escape.

"Can he leave the museum?" I asked.

"No," said Winnie's small voice. "But he's going to be really angry once he gets out."

Taylor's eyes darted around the room. "Who said that?"

Winnie made herself visible, startling Taylor so badly he almost fell off the box. "Your friend made it outside," she said. "I'll keep a hold of Charlie while you go join him. That way he can't hurt you."

"Thank you, Winnie. Thank you for helping us," I said.

"Can you do me a favor?" she said.

"Of course, what do you need?" I asked.

"Take Spooky with you. I don't want Charlie to hurt him. His claws don't hurt me, but they work on Spooky. Just take good care of him, wherever you go."

"Oh Winnie, I can't take your cat from you!"

"I told you," she said, "he's not mine. He's not anyone's." Before I could protest, she threw all her weight onto the box and disappeared.

"Go!" her voice chided as a phantom hand pushed me away. Taylor and I scrambled to our feet. A terrified Spooky was cowering in the corner, afraid of all the commotion. I scooped him up and chased after Taylor to the slide, where we rocketed to the first floor and bolted out the door. Just as we left, I heard a mad scream and the splintering of wood as Charlie broke out of his box. But thanks to Winnie, he couldn't stop us.

SARAH

We dashed out the door to see Tay furiously punching the keys on the flip phone while Mothman stood in front of him with the cross in his arms.

"Scree!" cried Mothman, his red eyes brightening and something resembling a smile forming on his buggy mouth. Tay finished up his message to Drake and slipped the phone back into his pocket. He turned around to see us and jumped back at the sight of Spooky cradled in my arms.

"That thing!" he cried. "Why do you still have it!?" I sighed. It looked like I was going to have to explain who Winnie was after all.

"Let's head back to the hotel and pack up," I said, gesturing down the sidewalk. "I'll explain on the way."

I told Tay and Taylor the full story of how I'd met Spooky and Winnie. I told them that the creature that hid behind the cross was Charlie the Imp, and that the reason he stayed in the box was because Winnie was holding him down.

"She wanted me to take Spooky with us," I explained. I held the cat against my chest as we passed by a group of humanoid lizard-people chatting in an alien language on the corner. One of them caught my eye and waved. I waved back, only because I was afraid I'd anger the monster if I didn't. I shifted Spooky in my arms.

"Winnie was worried Charlie would hurt him." Spooky looked up at me and pawed at a stand of my hair blowing in the wind.

"So we're just stuck with... *that* now?" Tay asked. "How long are we going to keep it? How do we feed it?"

"I'll find a pet store and get some supplies. I've owned a cat before; I can take care of him," I said, "at least until we can get back to

Area 51. Drake or one of the other trios can keep him as a pet from there."

"Come on, Tay," Taylor said, "we can't just leave him here."

Tay mumbled something under his breath. "Fine!" he grumbled.

Taylor directed us down a side street. "There's a pet store down this way, we might as well stop."

"Thank you," I said.

We followed Taylor a few blocks down the street (and we walked past what I could have sworn was a unicorn) to a pet supply shop. I picked out some canned food, cat litter and a small litter box, and a water bowl. Spooky sat obediently by my feet until Taylor bent down to pet him. The cat then trotted off to purr and rub his body around Taylor's ankles, having made a new friend.

Taylor carried Spooky back to the hotel lobby and I carried the supplies, while Tay, after finally chilling out about our new feline friend, strolled behind us, hands in his pockets.

Taylor put Spooky down in a lounge area in a corner of the lobby and I opened a can of food for him while Tay rearranged and repacked our bags, including the cat supplies. Spooky excitedly dove into his food as soon as I set it down in front of him, devouring the dish with speed and intensity.

"Wow," Tay said, "it was hungry."

"He probably only ate rats and table scraps from trashcans before," I said, "just look at how skinny he is."

We watched Spooky polish off his meal. Tay pulled the phone out of his pocket and called Drake.

"Hello?" Drake asked. "Mothman hasn't arrived with your cross yet. Is something wrong?"

"No, we just have some down time. We did get the cross, though, and Mothman's on his way," Tay said.

"Good, good," Drake mused.

"We found a cat!" Taylor quipped.

Drake paused. "I beg your pardon?"

"I met a ghost at the museum, and she wanted us to take her cat. She was worried it was in danger," I explained.

Drake was silent again, trying to comprehend what we were trying to tell him, "So... it's a ghost cat?"

"No, a real cat," I said. "He's hairless and a little beat up, but he's a real cat."

"His name is Spooky!" Taylor exclaimed.

"A real cat?" Drake questioned. "And not a feline-like monster or mystical being?"

I exchanged questioning glances with Tay and Taylor. I hadn't thought of that...

I looked down at Spooky again, who was kneading his paws into the carpet. He was hairless, beat up, and just a little bit ugly, but I knew cats, and he had the right body structure, the right behaviors, and even made the right sounds. He sure seemed like a cat to me.

"We'll send you a picture. You tell us," Tay said. I looked to him with gratitude. That was some smart thinking.

"But I really do think it's a real cat," I said.

"Fair enough," Drake said, "sometimes animals are pulled into this reality in animal trios or alongside human ones, or they slip through the layers in other ways. But I would like to verify that the animal isn't dangerous before you get in a car or plane with it."

The thought of animal trios saddened me. Had there been two other little hairless cats living in Spooky once, only for them to be electrified away and then die in a layer far from their home?

"Before you hang up, I'll inform you of your next mission. I want you to visit the Winchester Mystery House in San Jose, California, and take the sheets from Sarah Winchester's bed."

"Hey, that's not too far from my hometown," Tay remarked with a half-smile.

"Yes, I know. That's why I assigned this to you. Don't forget to send me that picture. Good luck." He ended the call.

Tay took a quick picture of Spooky and sent it to Drake. *Most likely a real cat*, Drake responded, *but be careful.*

"Alright," Tay said, "let's get on a shuttle to the airport. This boy's ready to head back home."

We picked up Spooky and our backpacks, got on a hotel shuttle bus, and were headed for the airport within fifteen minutes, California bound.

We arrived at the St. Louis airport in about half an hour. Taylor gazed out the window the whole time, silently saying goodbye to his home. We carried our kitty and our backpacks off the bus and into the airport, dodging crowds of people to get to a flight schedule and find the next plane to San Jose. We wandered for about ten minutes before we found one, but luckily the flight left in only an hour and the gate wasn't very far. We found it quickly and stopped to rest for a bit. Tay went to bring us lunch while Taylor and I stayed and played with Spooky. Taylor drummed his fingers on the carpet and Spooky pawed at them, and I let Spooky bat at my hair, too. Tay came back with food and we ate swiftly, talking very little. As soon as we were done, it was time to get on the plane.

We sat on the floor like we usually did, and once the plane's doors shut and there was no way to exit, I set Spooky down and let him wander. Taylor did some wandering too, before coming back with a set of colored pencils and a sketch pad. "Anybody want to play Pictionary?" he asked. "It's about a four-hour flight."

We each took a turn drawing something while the other two guessed what it was. Tay's drawings were of simple objects: a chair, a fish, a teapot. I tried to draw some animals, but they weren't very good and Tay and Taylor kept confusing them for other things. Taylor's drawings were more complex – a stained glass window, the Mona Lisa, the New York skyline – but he was a good artist, and it wasn't too hard to guess what he drew. Spooky came back to us about an hour later and curled up in my lap, fast asleep.

"That's not a bad idea, little guy," Tay said, "I'm gonna hit the hay too." He leaned against the wall and shut his eyes. Taylor flipped to a new page of the sketch book and kept drawing for fun. I patted

Spooky on the head and stared at the seat in front of us, wishing for a chair of my own.

The thought struck me that I had never been this far from home before. Grandma hardly ever left New England, so I never got to very often either. I'd been to Washington DC on a school trip, and Grandma and I had visited some distant family in western Pennsylvania, but Area 51 was much farther than both of those, and San Jose was even farther than that. The thought of the distance made me a little nervous, but then I remembered I didn't have a home to return to. I was supposed to be living with my cousin now. *Oh goodness, how long had I been in this layer of reality, almost a week now?* My cousin was probably losing her mind trying to find me, with a missing person's report filed and everything. I knew she didn't care about me very much, but she must have been at least a little concerned when the child she was supposed to be taking care of had vanished. What if they suspected her of murder? What if she suspected someone else of murder? How was I supposed to explain to her where I'd been when I showed up at her doorstep days, weeks, months, or even years from now? Would she even still take me in after all this, or would she be deemed unfit to care for children and have both me and her toddler taken from her by CPS and then her life would be ruined even though she had done nothing wrong and it was totally out of her control and my control and her daughter's control and—

Taylor slid a piece of paper onto my lap, resting it gently on top of Spooky like a blanket. It was a sketch of three gray shadow-figures standing beside one another. One had a scruffy blonde beard with a guitar slung across his back and a keyboard under his arm, the next stood wearing a nurse's coat and hat, and the final one wore a painting smock with colorful paint stains all over it.

"It's us," Taylor said, "it's what we want to be."

"It's beautiful," I said, picking up the paper to examine it more closely. It was a rough sketch, but it really was breath taking. I tried to hand the paper back to him, but he shook his head.

"I want you to have it. I don't like to keep anything I make." Normally I would have just accepted the paper, but it was such a gorgeous and unique drawing that I felt bad.

"Taylor, it's so beautiful, why don't you want it?"

"Because every piece of art I make is something I see in my mind. I'll have a copy of it forever in my head. The only reason I draw is so that I can share my visions with others." He smiled. "And because it's fun."

There he went again with his fantastic mind. He wasn't the typical type of genius, but he was, in his own way, one of the most brilliant people I knew.

"That's lovely, Taylor," I said. "Thank you."

He smiled and turned back to his sketchbook. I watched him doodle for a while, but my eyelids started to feel heavy. It was still hours until nightfall, but stealing the cross had been a lot of work. Within minutes of shutting my eyes, I was asleep.

I woke up just as the plane was taxying and people were starting to squirm in their seats, anxious to unbuckle their seat belts and rush into the airport. I peeked out a window to see that it was dusk, the sun turning the sky orange as it sank below the horizon. The plane reached the gate, and we walked through the people pulling their bags out of the overhead compartments and out the door into the airport.

The night air was cooler than I expected. I had always imagined California in the summertime would be warm no matter the time of day. We stepped outside to stalk the taxis for someone heading to a hotel, and the air was cold enough to make me hug Spooky's warm body tighter as I tried not to shiver.

"Tay, isn't California supposed to be warmer than this?" I finally asked. He smirked.

"In the South, yeah. This ain't Hollywood. No beaches and endless sunshine up here." He saw the goosebumps on my arms and added, "Don't worry, it's not so cold during the day. It's just not a giant beach like people think."

We saw a young couple who were asking a driver if he could take them to a hotel downtown, and we dashed to get into the backseat of the cab. This unfortunately involved Tay sitting in the husband, since the wife took the front seat and the cab only had the one back row. He went right through the man, of course, but he still looked very uncomfortable with the whole situation.

Fortunately, it wasn't a very long drive to the hotel. We got out of the car and into the lobby, waited for the couple to check in, then followed them up to their room. We set down our bags and set up our blankets. Tay wandered over to the window, staring at the highway outside.

"Have you been here before?" I asked. "To San Jose, I mean." He shook his head.

"No, I've never really left San Francisco before this."

"You didn't go on any vacations or field trips or have to visit someone who lived faraway?" I asked in disbelief. He'd really never left one city in his entire fifteen years of life?

"No, my parents weren't really the type to take me places. And there have always been a bunch of other kids in all my foster homes, and taking trips with five or ten kids is pretty expensive. And there's a lot going on within the city, so all our field trips were to somewhere downtown. We didn't really have that many, though," he said.

"Oh," I said, embarrassed that I had miscalculated the conditions he grew up in. "I'm sorry."

"Don't be," he responded, "I grew up in the greatest city in the world. I never wanted anything else."

The way he talked about it made me want to visit San Francisco, with its thriving downtown and shark-filled bays. I wanted to see where Tay grew up; I had gotten to see Taylor's hometown, after all.

The couple in the real layer turned off the lights, and Tay retreated from the window to crawl under his bedsheets. I slid into my make-shift bed as well, and I tilted my head to see Spooky snuggled up beside a sleeping Taylor.

"Good night," Tay said.

"Good night," I said.

I woke up the next morning to a low "mrrrrrooow" and the weight of Spooky sitting on my chest.

"Hi, buddy," I murmured, reaching up to pet his hairless head. He jumped off of me and I got up and fed him. He happily ate the entire can of food while I took a shower and changed into fresh clothing. I stepped out of the bathroom to find Taylor awake and waiting his turn while Tay still lied on the floor. I bent down beside him to check on his wolf bite and changed the bandage once more. He woke up as soon as I started doing so.

"Stay there for a bit," I told him, "I need to put a new bandage on it." He complied wordlessly, and Spooky slowly snuck over to his face and sniffed it cautiously. He playfully swatted the kitty away, but Spooky was back soon enough.

I studied Tay's bite: it was nasty, not because it was infected, but because the wolf had really torn into him, leaving several scabbing, half-healed fang holes. He was going to have a scar there for a long time. I cleaned his arm with an alcohol swab from the first aid kit in my bag, and he startled at the cold, looking back at his arm to see what I was doing to him.

"Hey, what was— whoa." He stared at his arm silently, examining the jagged scabby bite marks that covered it. "Dang," he whispered.

"I know it looks bad now, but it's going to heal," I told him.

"Yeah?" he said.

"Yeah," I confirmed.

He shrugged. "You're the doctor. Kind of."

Taylor came out of the bathroom and Tay went to take his turn after I finished caring for his arm. We played with Spooky until he was done, and then we went downstairs with our backpacks to eat breakfast and plan.

I took a map of the city from the brochure rack and we studied it over some orange juice and muffins. "It doesn't look *too* far," Taylor mused, "It would be a long walk, but we can do it."

Tay ran a hand through his hair. "Yeah, I don't think there's a simpler way."

"Works for me," I said.

"Do either of you know the story of this place?" Taylor asked, distracting me from what appeared to be a small dragon outside of our window. The monsters here differed in variety from the ones in St. Louis.

"I think I saw something about it on TV a while back," Tay said. "Basically, this lady, Sarah Winchester, her husband invented the Winchester rifle, which was used in the Civil War and killed a bunch of people. But her husband and daughter both died young, so she went to a psychic to see what was up. He told her that the ghosts of the people who had been killed by Winchester rifles were angry with her, and he told her that she needed to go and build a giant maze-type confusing house so that the ghosts would get lost and couldn't kill her too. He told her that if she ever stopped building, she would die. So she just kept building and building, and now the house is so weird and crazy they've turned it into a tourist trap."

"Wow," I said. Someone really had enough money, time, and patience to just build a house forever? It was hard to imagine being that afraid of ghosts.

"Did she die?" Taylor asked.

"She must have, because that was over a hundred years ago," Tay said. He stood up and stacked our empty plates and glasses. "Time to get walking," he said. We followed him out the door.

We walked past city buildings, traffic jams, and even more dragons until we came across a sprawling yellow mansion with a red roof. It was pretty, with lots of windows and a garden out front. I would have thought it was the house of some rich entrepreneur or movie star if I didn't know better.

We followed groups of tourists through the front door and into a normal-looking parlor. We skirted around the admissions desk and walked forward into the living room. It was grand, elegant, and beautiful, with oak paneling and red and golden wallpaper, a quaint red brick fireplace, and a beautifully carved upright organ.

Taylor and I stopped, looking around the room in awe. The organ started playing and I jumped before I realized it was Tay sitting at the keys, not a ghost. He played a quick tune that sounded classical and complicated. He played it beautifully, whatever the name of it was. He finished the song and turned to us, taking a silly, over the top bow. Taylor clapped and called, "Bravo!"

"How did you learn to play like that?" I asked.

He shrugged. "It's just what I've always done."

We left the living room in search of Sarah's blue bedroom, which was supposed to be right in the heart of the house. I could easily see why Sarah thought ghosts couldn't reach her there; the house was so full of dead ends and wrong turns and secret doors that we struggled to find the way. We managed to get ourselves completely lost in the polished wood rooms and corridors, barely aware of which way was up. We stopped walking to try and figure out our surroundings. "Okay," Tay said, "so we entered this hallway from that way—"

"No, it was from that way," Taylor insisted, pointing in the other direction.

"No, it had to be the other way," Tay said, but I thought they were both wrong.

"It was actually that way," I said, pointing behind us.

Tay groaned. "Ugh, never mind! Let's just walk until we find a tour group again." That wasn't a bad idea in principle, but the tours didn't go everywhere in the house, and we had left the tourists behind a long time ago.

"I don't think the tours go to her bedroom." I said.

He groaned again. "Okay, let's just keep going forward."

Tay, Taylor, and Spooky headed farther down the hall, and I tried to follow them, I really did, but this plan was intercepted when the floor fell out from beneath my feet. A trapdoor. I had no time to scream before I found myself plummeting down a long metal chute.

"Lori!" I heard Tay cry, but it was too late. I was plunged into darkness as the door shut above me. The chute ended almost as soon as it began, and I tumbled out of a wall and into a new room.

It was a quaint little kitchen, with an ice box from the late eighteen-hundreds and a mahogany counter. A ghost stood behind it, an elderly woman with short white hair, little brown eyes, and a beautiful yet weathered face. She wore a big, elaborate brown dress and a little brown felt hat with three chicken feathers sewn into the side.

"Goodness gracious, that was quite the entrance, my dear. Are you alright?" she asked. I was still dazed from my sudden tumble, but I nodded. The woman clicked her tongue and murmured, "Oh, my, my, my!" I pushed myself off the ground and dusted myself off, and she cleared her throat. "Well, I've been expecting you," she said. "My name is Sarah Winchester, and yours is Lori. You're an orphan, I do adore orphans." I looked up at the spirit again. Wait, was this *the* Sarah Winchester? And how did she know my name? And that my parents were dead?

"How did you—"

"Come, help yourself to some ice cream, my dear," she interrupted, gesturing to two pink and white ceramic bowls on the table. "We have much to talk about."

*****

Before I knew it, I was sitting on a pretty wooden stool behind a pretty wooden counter, eating ice cream while the ghost of Sarah Winchester sat across from me, lovingly watching me with her head resting on her hand. "Oh, I do love orphans," she sighed. The ice cream was vanilla, but it was the old fashioned homemade kind that they give you in summer camps or after church, the kind that tastes more like a gentle, icy sweetness than raw vanilla extract. I had only had a spoonful, but I instantly knew I was going to finish the whole bowl with no trouble. But I stopped myself before picking up my spoon again. I had questions to ask. "So..." I began cautiously, looking up from my bowl. "You said you were expecting me. Why?"

"You're in this layer, but you're no supernatural goddess or ghost," Sarah said. "You're from the real layer. I could tell that as soon as you set foot in my house."

"That's true," I said, "my friends and I are trying to get home."

"But then why are you here, my dear?" asked Sarah. "I take it you don't live *here* in the real layer."

"No, I live in Concord. Well, I guess Providence now. But we need your bedsheets."

Sarah looked aghast. "My bedsheets? Dear my, that's quite scandalous."

"Oh no no, it's not like that!" I said quickly. I had forgotten she had lived during a much more conservative time period. "This is going to sound crazy," I started, "but a scientist is extracting power from objects that exist within all layers. He thinks your bedsheets are special, and he wants us to get them for him. We've been getting objects for him all week so he can use their power to cast a spell and get us home."

"I believe you, dearie," she said, "I know all about those universal objects, but I never guessed my bedsheets would be one! I suppose it's because I died on them."

"Oh," I said, not sure how to respond to that.

"But when you say scientist," she continued, "you surely don't mean that awful man with the wolf's face."

"No!" I said. "We're working against him; he's the one who's been disrupting everything."

She sighed. "He most certainly has been disrupting things." She looked straight into my eyes, her warm gaze replaced with something sadder, more serious. "I could tell something has been off for the past few days," she said. "A storm has been brewing, and it's about to hit. Something serious is about to happen with him, but I can't tell if it will be the end of his mess, or the end of all of us."

Her words chilled me. I had felt like something was off too, ever since the shift in layers. Conan was getting stronger, and his conflicts with us were about to reach a boiling point. I was starting to feel like I had been pulled into the layers of the Unreal just before the climax of the war.

"I can't leave this house, not anymore." Sarah said. "But my dear, you cannot let this man win. If he gets to the farthest layer, we'll be brought with him, and nothing will be able to survive as it has."

A lump formed in my throat. I knew how much danger we were in, but hearing Sarah remind me of it somehow made me feel like crying. "I know," I said weakly, "I know."

"He visited here about two years ago," she said. "He didn't take my bedsheets, but he did take my old spirit board. He didn't notice at the time, but this fell out of his pocket."

She produced a small, simple wooden box with a flower engraved on the lid. I opened it up and the box sprung to life. A little white, glass flower bud spun in a circle, while a piano version of the song "Edelweiss" from *The Sound of Music* played. It was a music box. But why did Conan own this?

"Flip it over," Sarah instructed. I did, and on the bottom of the box was a little note written on the wood in pen. *To my very own Captain von Trapp. With love, VNW*

"It was a gift from his fiancée," Sarah said. "You do know that he's doing all this to find her and his brother, don't you? He lost them in a car accident. He was driving, and he couldn't forgive himself."

I had known all this about Conan because of Drake, but the music box humanized him. It made me feel empathy, empathy I didn't want to have. Conan was endangering the very fabric of the universe with no consideration to the beings within it, but he was grieving, grieving for his fiancée and brother that he loved so dearly. He was grieving, just like I was.

"He came back to look for it, but I hid it from him," Sarah said.

"Why?" I asked. Sarah was such a sweet old lady, and even though Conan was a villain to her, taking a memento he carried to remember his dead fiancée seemed unnecessarily cruel.

Sarah leaned in close to me. "He forgets that he's human. He's gotten so deep into this endeavor that he's lost all sight of where he came from. That's why I wanted to talk to you. I want you to take this, so that when you see him, you can remind him that he's still a human, just like his dead family members."

I slipped the pretty little music box into my pocket. "Thank you, Sarah," I said. "I'll do whatever I can."

I began to hear voices outside the walls, voices that were calling my name. Tay and Taylor. Oh no, they were probably worried sick about me! They had no idea where I'd gone!

"It sounds like your friends are looking for you," Sarah said. "My bedroom is just down the hall, the third door on the right." A door on the left side of the room opened.

"Wait, can't you show me? I'm scared I'll get lost again."

"No, honey, you're the only person I want to see today. You have a gift, Lori, a gift that is unique among both your friends and your enemies."

Something was telling me that by "gift" she didn't mean Conan's music box. I started to ask her what she was talking about, but she quickly cut me off. "Hurry now, third door on the right. There are no trapdoors in this hallway, I promise." She winked and began shooing me towards the door.

"Thank you again, Sarah," I said. "You've helped me so much."

"Be careful out there," she said, "a storm is about to strike." She didn't need to remind me. I could feel it. "And when the time comes," she said, "do not let him win. Remind him that he's human."

Sarah disappeared into thin air behind me, leaving behind nothing but the scent of lavender and two unfinished bowls of vanilla ice cream.

I walked out the door to the kitchen and bumped right into Taylor. "Lori!" he and Tay both cried, enveloping me in a huge group hug. Spooky ran circles around our feet, purring with glee.

"Where have you been?" Tay asked.

"I fell down a trap door that lead to that kitchen," I explained, "I met Sarah Winchester's ghost. She said her bedroom is right down here." I walked down the hallway and opened the third door on the right, and sure enough, the room inside was a blue bedroom with a great canopy bed in the center, covered with Sarah's bedsheets. Both boys gasped in astonishment.

"We found them!" Taylor cried with joy. "We finally found them!"

"Dang," Tay remarked, "how come Lori always meets all the ghosts?" Sarah's words echoed in my mind. *You have a gift...*

Tay and I pulled the blankets off the bed while Taylor rounded up Spooky. Triumphant, we began our journey out of the maze of a house.

SAN FRANCISCO

Finding our way out of the house was much easier than I expected it to be. We worked our way back to the front parlor in less than fifteen minutes. A part of me blamed the increased tourist rush and the fact that we had been to the parlor before, but I also had a feeling that Sarah's ghost was guiding us, helping us continue on our way and get ever closer to facing Conan. The music box was heavy in my pocket, a grim reminder of what I was going to have to do. I knew I was going to see him again, and this time, things would be serious.

We walked outside into the warm California sunlight and summoned Mothman. Tay checked the time on our cellphone; it was only 2:30.

"What now?" he asked. "We've still got time before the great moth arrives." From looking up and down the street, there didn't seem to be many other tourist attractions nearby, so we got lunch at a restaurant a few blocks away. We sat at an outdoor table with some hamburgers and fries, and Spooky chowed down on his cat food by our feet. Tay and Taylor wanted to know what else Sarah had told me. I frowned at my food.

"Do you guys... do you feel like something's been wrong lately?" I asked. Tay gestured all around us.

"You mean the fact that we're in a different layer of reality than we should be and that there are ghosts and dragons and other monsters all around us and that there's an evil dude trying to bring everyone into a reality filled with literally everything that doesn't exist? Cause yeah, I'd say that feels pretty wrong."

I scowled at him. "I mean; do you feel like something bad is about to happen? Like, all of this," I imitated the gesture that Tay had made, "is about to come to a head." Both Tay and Taylor stopped eating then, their faces suddenly serious.

"Actually," Taylor said, "I have."

"I thought I was just being paranoid," Tay said.

"Well, Sarah felt that way too," I said, "she told me a storm was brewing. Like we're close to the breaking point, where we'll either go home or go to the layer of the Unreal. Where we'll have to face Conan in a life or death manner."

Our table was silent, all three of us contemplating that matter. I didn't feel ready to confront our enemy yet; we'd barely been here a week. But part of my anxiety came from the fact that I wasn't ready to go home yet either, to face my new life with my cousin in Providence. My life in this layer sure wasn't pretty, but the longer I stayed in it the longer I wasn't facing the immediate future I dreaded.

I considered telling Tay and Taylor about the music box, but like Conan's statements about my love for my grandma, it felt too personal to share. The conversation of grief was something between only me and Conan; something I had to confront him about by myself.

Our dreadful thoughts were interrupted by a low yowl below the table. Spooky had polished off his food, and was eyeing Taylor expectantly. He broke off a piece of meat from his hamburger and fed it to the cat, who tore it from his hand and gobbled it up in one excited bite. He jumped up on Taylor's lap, begging for more meat with his big, green eyes. Taylor gave Spooky another table scrap, which he ate just as excitedly. It was a funny sight; the skinny, hairless cat sitting at the table like a toddler on his mother's lap, and we couldn't help but laugh.

"You're a silly kitty," Taylor said, patting Spooky on the head and offering him a French fry, which the cat gratefully accepted. We laughed again, and I felt better.

"Listen," I said to them, "whatever happens with Conan, happens. If we get to go home like we want, then great. But if we don't..." I looked at my friends, hoping my words could somehow reassure them. "Then we'll find a way to adapt."

Tay smiled. "Or, you know, we'll die in the process, so we won't be able to worry about it."

Taylor erupted in laughter, and I tried my hardest to suppress my giggles as I smacked Tay's elbow. "You have a dark, dark sense of humor," I said.

He smiled and shrugged his shoulders. "What else can I do?" he said. "These are dark, dark times." He had a point.

We finished up our meal, with Spooky stealing bits of meat whenever he got the chance. Mothman came rocketing over to us and snatched up the orange we had left for him at the corner of the table. I had learned better than to leave it underneath the table again. He devoured the snack, we texted Drake and handed our mothy friend the blankets, and he flew away, en route to Area 51. The cellphone buzzed with a call from Drake. Tay put it on speakerphone and answered it. "Hel—"

"Your next location will be on Alcatraz Island in the San Francisco bay." Drake interrupted, "I trust you secured the blankets with little trouble."

"Could've said hello back," mumbled Tay, too quietly for Drake to hear.

"We got a little lost, but Mothman has them." Taylor assured him.

"Good, good. Well, I'm going to need you to take a mug from Cell 68-C. It's connected with a legend of a ghost of man who tried to escape the island but failed. Ferries leave for the island every half an hour, so you should have no trouble getting to the prison. It's in an out-of-the-way area, so as long as no one drops the cup no one will notice it's gone."

"Okay!" Taylor said. "We can do that."

"Good."

"Drake?" I asked.

He paused for a moment. "Yes, Lori?"

I wasn't quite sure how to ask my question, but I tried anyway. "Are things... about to be over? Is something about to happen between us and Conan?"

Drake was silent for a long time. Then, "Children, I can't say. But whatever happens... I'll let you know." And with that, he hung up the phone.

We grabbed our bags and our cat and left the table in silence, worried about what Drake had said. He'd never outright admit it, but he sounded nervous, like he knew more than he was letting on. But I knew I couldn't worry about his words for long, because we had more immediate problems at hand. "How are we getting to San Francisco?" I asked. Tay pointed at the house's parking lot.

"Most of the people there are probably vacationing in San Fran, but just decided to take a day trip up here. Almost any car we hitch a ride in will take us back to the city."

"But how can we be sure?" I asked.

Tay smiled. "Come with me, friends," he said, "I'm going to teach you how to spot a tourist."

We stood near the front door of the house in the middle of the parking lot while Tay examined each and every person that came outside. He pointed people out to us as we waited. "See that lady? Local history buff. She's the type that comes here almost every weekend and volunteers in the local cemeteries. That type doesn't make much, so she'd be hard pressed to afford an apartment by the bay."

He pointed to a family with three young kids. "Those people are the road trippers. See how tired the parents are and that Minnesota license plate? They could be heading to San Francisco next, or they could have just come from there. We shouldn't risk it."

A teenaged couple came out next. "They're too young to be on vacation by themselves. Most likely locals here on a date. They could live anywhere from the heart of the city to way out in the suburbs, though, so we shouldn't go with them."

He went on like that for a while, trying to determine our best bet to San Francisco. I was amazed at how he could sort people so well, but I guess after living in a big city all his life, he'd seen just about every type of person on the planet.

"There!" he cried excitedly, pointing to a middle-aged couple carrying cameras and wearing matching sweatshirts with the Golden Gate Bridge on them. "They're definitely going back to the city."

We climbed into their car and found a pile of roadmaps and brochures pushed into one seat. "Oh yeah, definite tourists," he said. "They bought those sweatshirts 'cause they didn't realize the bridge was going to be so cold. And they've got all those maps because they don't know the area well."

Listening to Tay was like watching a real-life Sherlock Holmes in action, and because of that I completely trusted his deductions. Sure enough, the couple drove off onto a highway that, according to the roadmaps, was taking us right into the city.

All three of us watched the world pass by through the windows, excited to reach our new destination. Taylor was filled with questions, all of which Tay had the answers to.

"Will we go over the Golden Gate Bridge?" Taylor asked.

"Not from this direction," Tay said, "we're coming to the city from the southeast."

"Oh," Taylor said, sounding a little disappointed. "What about that street with all the turns?"

"Lombard Street? You have to wait at least an hour to go down it, it's really more of a tourist thing than an actual road."

"Oh."

"What about those leopard sharks?" I teased. "Can you show them to us?"

Tay laughed. "I can try; we'll be taking a boat to Alcatraz." His face brightened with an idea. "Oh, you guys will love this! On Pier 41, there are these sea lions that lay on near the docks all day. Like, at least fifty of them, all crammed onto two or three wooden docks in the ocean. And then a new sea lion will come along and start climbing over all the others, and it's just so funny and cute, oh man, you guys will love it. And it's right by the aquarium, too!" I smiled at the thought of the snuggling sea lions, and at how happy Tay got when he talked about his city. I was starting to see how he was satisfied with never leaving.

Slowly but certainly, the tips of skyscrapers became visible in the distance as the sun dropped in the sky. They were taller than anything I'd ever seen before – we certainly didn't have skyscrapers in Concord, and St. Louis wasn't quite this big, either. As we edged closer to the city, Tay tapped on my window.

"Look out there," he whispered, pointing to the horizon. The Golden Gate Bridge loomed over the fog of the ocean, and the sight of it took my breath away. There it was, possibly the most famous landmark in the whole country, a bridge I had seen in pictures and in books for all my life, but now I was seeing it for real and realizing that, as cliché as it sounded, that the pictures really didn't do it justice. It was so much longer than I imagined, and the sinking sun turned it a gorgeous shade of red.

Soon the skyscrapers enveloped us, and we were driving down the streets of San Francisco, passing by fancy hotels, public parks, and houses where all the other stories were stacked on top of a garage that faced out into the street. "I live in a house like that," Tay told me. "It's not in this area, but it's that design."

Sure enough, the couple pulled into the parking garage of a chain hotel located close to downtown. We got out of the car and followed them to their hotel room, where we put down our bags and Spooky. We had barely gotten settled before Tay stood leaning against the room's door with his hand on the doorknob, waiting for us to join him.

"Where are we going? It's seven in the evening," Taylor said. Tay smiled.

"Sightseeing," he said. "There's something I want to show you."

Tay assured us that we'd love it and that we'd only be gone for a couple of hours, so we followed him, deciding Spooky would be safe in the room. He led us out down the hallway and out of the lobby, then looked left and right down the street. "We're pretty close to the docks," he said, turning left. "That means it's this way."

"*What's* that way?" I prodded.

"A hiding spot."

We walked further down the city streets, past brightly colored condo buildings, the occasional trolley car, and streets that slanted upwards at seemingly impossibly steep angles. Walking up and down them made my legs turn sore quickly, especially because I could feel the soreness in Tay and Taylor's legs, too.

Tay would stop at a corner, look around carefully, then led us down yet another side street. We walked for what felt like forever. It was dark now, and I was about to tell Tay that I was ready to head back when he stopped in front of a mostly abandoned, heavily graffitied sky-blue apartment building.

"This is it," he said, walking to the side of the house, pulling himself on top of a dumpster, and climbing up the fire escape. He helped me up too, but Taylor took the moment to practice his flying skills. He fluttered over the dumpster and onto the fire escape to join us in climbing up the ladder.

I followed Tay to the rooftop and gasped. The roof itself held nothing of note, but the view around it was breathtaking. From one direction the skyscrapers of downtown glistening in the near distance. Behind and to the left of me was a clear view of the shimmering ocean and the Golden Gate Bridge. To the right of us, way in the distance, stood a range of purpling mountains. Directly in front of us was a tall, white tower that resembled a candle stick. Tay pointed to it.

"Coit Tower," he said. Right then, he could have told me it was called anything and it would've sounded beautiful.

The whole city glistened and shown like the lights of a Christmas tree, and the it blended flawlessly with the ocean and mountains around it. And in that moment, standing on the rooftop of a stranger's apartment with two of my favorite people in the universe, staring out at a city I had just come to know, I felt like the whole world was perfect and right. It was the most beautiful thing I'd ever seen.

"Tay, it's... it's..." I couldn't finish the thought. What words could describe it? Tay laughed and smiled at his feet.

"I know," he said. Taylor was absolutely mesmerized, turning his head to look left, right, left, behind, right; he couldn't decide what merited his attention, and I felt for him. It was all so beautiful, it was hard to decide what to watch.

"Tay, how did you find this place?" I asked. He smiled, but this time his eyes didn't smile along with him.

"I have little safe spots like this picked out all over the city," he said. "Sometimes, I just didn't want to be at home, so..." his voice trailed off and he gestured at the landscape around us. "So I'd go somewhere else." He looked down at the sidewalk, his smile gone, as he remembered.

A vision came to my own mind, one of Tay, younger, more fearful, but still Tay, sprinting down the city sidewalks, breathing hard. He ran all the way to the very apartment we stood on, scampered up fire escape, and pulled himself up on the roof. He peered over the side of the building, panting, checking the roads for whatever had been chasing him. *Paul, it was Paul, a big balding man with a belt in one hand.* Tay was supposed to be referring to him as "Father" like the other boys did.

After far too many minutes of scanning the streets, Tay crashed onto the floor of the building, exhausted. He started to cry, big, heartbroken sobs. And there he cried, alone on this rooftop, a child too young to be crying alone in a huge metropolis by himself.

The vision vanished, and I looked to Tay, as he stood overlooking the same stretch of sidewalk, very possibly remembering the same memory I had seen. I was used to feeling my trio's physical pain, but my vision made me feel like I was sharing in Tay's mental pain as well. I stood beside him and put a hand on his shoulder.

"Did he hurt you?" I whispered. He looked at me briefly, tears welling up behind his eyes. I thought he was going to pull away and ask me who I thought "he" was, and I didn't know how I was going to respond. But instead he took a shaky breath and looked back down at the street.

"No," he said, "but... there were a couple of times when he tried to." He fidgeted with his shirt, avoiding my worried glance. "I wasn't the best kid," he said.

"But you were still a kid." I said, "Kids don't know any better. That doesn't justify abuse." I put my arm around him. He took another shaky breath.

"Yeah," he said. "Yeah. That's what I try to tell myself."

I leaned my head against his shoulder, and he rested his own head on mine, putting his arm around me too. We stood like that for a long time, watching the people and cars go by below us. Taylor eventually made his way to our side of the rooftop too, and he lay down, watching streets, the same way that young Tay had. I wondered if there was any chance he had seen Tay's memory, too. I knew he hadn't, but I hoped against hope he had. Despite what Sarah had told me, I didn't want to be the sole possessor of a ghost-calming, empathetic, telepathic power. I mean, sure, that was cool that I had a "special" ability or whatever, but it also put a lot of pressure on me. I would have died so many times this week alone if Tay and Taylor hadn't had my back. What would happen if I used my power at the wrong time, or I couldn't figure out how to use it when I really needed it?

We watched the streets until they were almost empty, when the pedestrians had long since gone to bed and there was only the occasional car. We watched the streets until Taylor turned his head to the left and said, "Whoa."

The city beside us had become brighter in the advancing darkness, lights in windows and on rooftops sparkling like a galaxy of stars in the night. Somehow, the city had become even more beautiful, and I felt like I was in love. Tay stepped away from me and walked over to the far edge of the roof top, his arms crossed, smiling at his city.

After a moment, he turned to us and said, "It's getting late. The first ferry leaves at 9 am. We should get some sleep." He climbed down the fire escape, and I reluctantly followed. Taylor stood on the roof for a bit longer, still hypnotized by the lights of the city, but he finally took a step off the roof and let his wings carry him down. Tay led us back to our hotel, and all three of us constantly turned our heads back towards the city lights as we walked until we could see them no more.

*****

I woke up the next morning to the robotic beeping of an alarm clock.

"Meow! ME-YOW!" cried Spooky, irritatedly swatting at the device with his paws. Tay groaned and fumbled to hit the snooze button. Taylor stood, stretched, and opened the curtains, filling the room with the too-bright morning sun and causing me to shield my eyes like a vampire at the beach. I reluctantly made my way out of bed and got ready in the bathroom. Then I sat on the bed in a still-tired trance while Tay and Taylor got ready too, Spooky purring anxiously around my feet.

We fed Spooky and ate a quick breakfast in the lobby, without planning like we usually did because Tay knew the way to the ferry and exactly when it left. We did decide to leave Spooky in the room again, however, because we'd be traveling by boat, and we were fairly certain that our kitty wouldn't do so well in water.

"Bye, Spookster," Taylor said as he plopped the cat down on the hotel room floor.

"Meow?" said Spooky.

"Come on," Tay said, checking the clock on the flip phone. "The ferry leaves in forty-five minutes." We followed him out of the hotel and let him lead us to Fisherman's Wharf, marked by a sign shaped like the captain's wheel of a boat and emblazoned with a crab. The area was crawling with an odd mix of seagulls, pigeons, and tourists. Tay led us down a long, seaside street lined with ornate white buildings with grand, arched entrances, with black lettering counting in odd intervals from Pier 35 all the way down to Pier 1. There were piers

41 and 39 too, but they looked more like a collage of shopping centers and tourist attractions than working shipping ports. One of them even had the aquarium Tay had mentioned. I pointed it out to him and asked if it was the one he had visited as a child. He smiled, "Yep, that's the one! Maybe we can visit if we have extra time..."

It took forever, but we eventually made it to a long, blueish building with a tall clock tower on top. Tay snapped his fingers and pointed.

"That's it!" he cried, picking up speed as he hurried us around to the right side of the building. A small dock lined with people stood before us, and a large ferry boat was tethered to the dock. We passed through the tourists and wobbled our way on board, climbed up to the second deck, and stood by the railing, peering over the ocean at the island that harbored possibly the most notorious prison in history.

Tay leaned further over the railing, looking straight into the sea, probably searching for leopard sharks. But instead of a shark, a huge, scaly sea serpent slithered under the dock, reminding us that we were still in a layer of reality far from our own. The boat started with a jolt, and soon we were off, sailing straight towards our next mission.

The boat ride took almost forty-five minutes, longer than I had expected. The island slowly became larger on the horizon, and I could make out the details of the prison that rested on top of it. A rusty water tower and smokestack towered above the island. A black and tan striped structure that resembled a parking garage stood on the close edge of the island, while a long white professional-looking building occupied the highest peak. It resembled a government building straight out of Washington DC, but I knew it housed the jail cells. That was where we'd be headed.

I kept my eyes on the horizon, trying to ignore the monstrous sea serpents that occasionally swam underneath the tiny ferry. The sight of the haunted prison freaked me out enough already.

The boat docked at the island, and we rushed past the slowly rising passengers to start climbing to the top of the island. There were even more seagulls here, and we even passed by a nest of fuzzy, speckled seagull chicks.

"Aw, look, baby seagulls!" I said, pointing out the family to my companions.

"Actually, we call them bay-gulls here," Tay said, "you know, because this is a bay, and a bagel is... it's a... oh, never mind. The tourists all think it's funny."

Speaking of tourists, a trolley train of them passed by us, traveling up the steep pathway to the prison. "Do you think we could get on one of those?" Taylor asked.

"We could," Tay responded, "if there was room." He was right, the trolleys were jam packed with people, and I wasn't in the mood to sit in anyone's lap.

"Come on, it's not that much higher," he assured us. Taylor and I shrugged. What else could we do but keep walking?

My feet complained and protested like never before, but we finally made it uphill to the main prison. We followed the flood of people inside to a long row of simple, well-aged jail cells, each painted a light green and yellow and stocked with a simple toilet, sink, and the remains of bed supports. One cell had the bed still attached, and a cluster of people around it. A crude plaster head poked out from under the covers, like a third-grade art project.

"Oh yeah, that was the room of one of the guys who escaped," Tay whispered. I frowned. Even by modern day standards, this jail seemed like it would be almost impossible to leave. Perhaps you could break out of the actual prison building, but getting over that stretch of ocean alone without a boat would be unimaginable.

"Three guys used those fake heads to trick the guards into thinking they were asleep after they chiseled their way out through those air vents," Tay explained, pointing to a hole in the wall and an air vent cover on the floor in front of it. "Then they made an inflatable boat out of rubber jackets and sailed away. No one knows what happened to them after that."

It was a daring attempt at freedom, but it was still hard for me to imagine three men surviving a voyage across that treacherous length of sea in a such a crude raft. Life here must have been excruciating for someone to be that desperate for freedom.

"That's neat," Taylor said, "but where's the cell we're looking for?"

Tay bit his lip and pointed upwards. "Top floor," he said. Two rows of identical cells were stacked on top of the first, with the third row a good forty feet in the air with no clear way up.

"They don't let anyone up there anymore," Tay said. I pursed my lips, thinking hard. If no one went up there, was it still properly maintained? Was it stable to walk on?

"Taylor, do you think you could fly up there?" I asked.

He looked up at the third floor, his face nervous as he saw how high up it was. "It would be farther up than I've ever flown before," he said, "but I can try."

"You can grab onto the railings on the second floor for a break," Tay suggested. "Then it'll only be twice as high a flight."

"That's a great idea!" I said. "And we can locate the exact cell from down here. Then you can just fly straight up, grab the mug, and come right back down again." Taylor paused for a moment, considering our ideas.

"Alright," he said, "I guess I'll give it a go."

"Awesome! Thanks, man," Tay said, clapping Taylor on the back.

"I promise we won't let you fall," I said.

Taylor gave us a wan smile. "Alright, where is it?"

Tay checked the phone and read a text from Drake that gave a more detailed description of the cell's location. "Cell block C, cell 58. We're in cell block A right now." He wandered down the aisle of jail cells and we followed him, hoping he knew where he was going better than we did.

The prison wasn't as big as I initially thought, and Tay located the right cell block with little trouble. He pointed at the third row, to the cell marked 58-C.

"There it— whoa," he stopped in his tracks as he read an informational display poster on the wall. "Oh, dang. I didn't know the mug was related to *this* escape attempt..."

"What is it?" I asked, examining the poster. *The Battle of Alcatraz, 1946,* read the heading. Below it were six pictures of former inmates along with a description of the event.

"This was a really famous escape attempt," Tay explained, "these six prisoners took over the weapons safe, killed some guards, and held the others hostage. They tried to take a boat out of here, but they couldn't get the ignition keys. The army had to come to stop all the chaos, and the three guys on top here died." He pointed to the top three inmate's portraits. He tilted his head up to the cell above us. "That's Bernard Coy's cell. He died in the battle."

I suddenly felt sick to my stomach. An angry prisoner killed in a violent escape attempt. It sounded like we could very well likely have to face off against another ghost, and something told me he wouldn't be kindred and helpful like Sarah or Winnie or open to negotiation like Mercy. I really hoped I wouldn't be the one he singled out to confront.

I looked to Taylor and saw that he had turned pale; he was just as nervous as I was, probably even more so. He extended his wings, stretching them out and readying them for flight. "Well," he said, his voice weak, "let's hope for the best."

With Tay and I cheering him on, he slowly fluttered up to the second floor bannister, grabbed onto it, and placed his feet between the railings, steadying himself on the second floor before starting his journey up to the third. He took a deep breath, flapped his wings harder, and pushed himself away from the bannister. He wobbled in air for a moment, but regained his balance and flew up to the third floor. I sighed with relief, beyond grateful that he hadn't fallen.

"Do you see the mug?" Tay called to him.

"Yeah!" he called back.

"Can you reach it through the bars?"

"Yeah!" Taylor pulled the mug through the bars and returned to the edge of the banister, raising it in the air triumphantly. Tay and I cheered again, and he flapped his wings and stepped off the edge of the railing, gently fluttering his way back down to us.

"Yes!" cried Tay, pumping his fist. "Aw man, that's the one!" The mug was a tin drinking cup with a crude tin handle; in other words, it was overly simple, exactly the kind of thing you'd expect to find in a prison.

"We should get out of here," Taylor said, his expression suddenly stoic. "You know, before something happens." The three of us nervously turned to look at the jail cell. Nothing seemed to be happening – no angry ghost glared at us from behind the cell bars – but we all knew better than to sit around waiting. I took off running for the exit, and Tay and Taylor sprinted after me.

We ran out the doors and towards the boat, this time thankful for the incline of the island because the downward slopes allowed us to run even faster with less effort. We bolted onto the ferry and collapsed, panting and gasping for breath. We glanced towards the entrance to the prison as we struggled for air, trying to determine if anyone, or anything, was following us. But as far as I could tell, the only thing coming out of the prison doors were more tourists.

"It. Looks. Like. We're. Safe." I sputtered in between gasping breaths. Tay pulled the phone out of his pocket and checked the time.

"We should be leaving in about five minutes," he said. "Let's hope nothing happens until then."

We sat down near the railing of the ship and obsessively stared at the doors of the prison until the boat's engine came to life and we drifted away from the island. We all sighed with relief. Unfortunately, we weren't so lucky as to escape scot-free like we had hoped.

Taylor yelped and pointed a shaking hand at the island. A figure in a pinstripe suit and fedora was sauntering away from the prison like he hadn't a care in the world. He caught our glances and waved, a twisted smile on his face. It was a face I recognized, a face that I had seen just moments before on a poster near the jail cell. Bernard Coy.

I screamed in terror as the dead convict strutted further down the pathway and towards our slowly sailing ferry. Tay clamped a hand over my mouth and let out a loud "SHH!"

"Calm down, we're not docked anymore," he said. "He's on the island, and we're at sea. He can't get us." I looked back at Bernard's ghost, who had now walked down to the dock and was staring at our departed boat. I took a deep breath and tried to relax a little. Tay was right, he had no way to get on our boat, and we were moving farther away from him by the second. I turned away from his haunting stare and tried to focus on the city in front of us. *We'll be there soon,* I thought to myself, *then we'll be completely safe. Nothing is going to happen.*

We were about halfway to the city when Taylor screamed and pointed at something behind the ferry. I looked at what he was pointing at and let out a scream of my own. Floating over the water behind us was Bernard's ghost, and it was advancing on the ship fast. Tay was screaming now too, and we all scrambled to our feet, terrified of what was going to happen but unsure of how to stop it.

Bernard floated onto the ferry's dock and strolled towards us, hands in his pockets, that same sick, cruel smile on his face. We could only scream louder and cling to each other as the ghost of a hardened criminal came closer and closer to us. We knew from our brief battle with Mercy that any punches we threw would go straight through him, but he could fight us as well as another living human, perhaps even better than any human could. And this time, there were no open spaces to run through, no graves to duck behind, no church to cower in.

When Bernard stood only a few feet from us, Tay's instincts took over. He took a swinging punch at the ghost, and to my immense surprise, it collided with his jaw as if he were made of real human flesh. Bernard blinked twice, looking just as stunned as we were, but his shock quickly turned to rage as he thrust a hand around Tay's throat. I froze, paralyzed with shock and terror and the pain from the hand closing around Tay's neck, but thankfully Taylor acted when Tay and I couldn't. He reeled back his foot and kicked Bernard's shin with all his might, causing the ghost to yelp and release his grip on Tay. He fell to the floor and Bernard turned his rage to Taylor, throwing a punch at his face that Taylor quickly dodged.

"HEY!" I yelled, fighting against my fear-induced paralysis. Bernard whipped his head around to me, holding Taylor by his shirt collar. But as soon as those crazed eyes met mine, I froze again. *Oh dear, what now? Do something, Lori, do anything!*

To my great relief, Tay pounced up from the floor and tackled Bernard to the ground. They wrestled on the deck, rolling around like brother and sister play-fighting over some petty disagreement. I saw the tin cup on the ground, dropped by Tay when he was being strangled, and got an idea of something I could do to help. I grabbed the cup and brought it down with all the force I could muster on Bernard's skull, striking him hard with an awful *clunk!* He yowled in pain and threw Tay off of him, struggling to get up and regain his balance. He wasn't a bad fighter, but it was three against one. We had him beat. Taylor gave Bernard another harsh kick to the shin, causing the ghost to lose his balance further, which Tay took advantage of to slam his shoulder into Bernard with all his might, sending him tumbling off the railing and into the frigid ocean below.

We stumbled our way over to the railing, looking out into the sea, checking to see if our attacker really was gone. There was no sight of him, and we finally fell to the floor, breathing hard.

"Is... is everyone okay?" I asked. Taylor started to say something, but the sound of a metallic screeching cut him off. The real-layer ferry and the real-layer people on it kept chugging on ahead in front of us, a ghostly figure sailing on down the remaining stretch of ocean to the city, but the boat in our layer had stopped moving, and smoke was coming up from somewhere below deck. Bernard appeared before us again, the sick smile back on his face.

"No one escapes the rock," he taunted, his voice cold and his smile crazed. Then he evaporated into thin air. The ship groaned and started slowly tipping to the left.

"Oh god, he did something to the engine and the hull! We're sinking!" Tay cried.

"What?!" I yelled in terror. I looked at the mainland: We were more than three fourths of the way there, but it still looked like an impossibly far distance away. Tay threw off his shoes and dug the cell phone out of his pocket and placed it in the mug. Taylor and I stood frozen, unsure of what to do in a shipwreck. Tay shouted at us.

"Don't just stand there!" he cried. "Leave your coats and shoes and anything that'll weigh you down! We're going to have to swim for it!"

"I can't swim!" I cried. I had lived with an old lady all my life, she never went to the pool and so neither did I. What good did swimming do me in a landlocked suburban town?

"I can't either!" Taylor panicked. Tay looked to both of us in shock.

"Are you kidding me? *Neither* of you can swim?" We shook our heads frantically, my head and heart filling with panic as the ship tilted and sunk further into the water. Tay let out an agitated moan and ran a hand through his hair. He darted into the cabin, rushing back with three life jackets, which he shoved into each of our arms before gingerly handing the mug to Taylor.

"Fly along with us for as long as you can, then gently lower yourself into the water. I'll get you to shore from there. Do *not* get those wet." Taylor nodded in understanding, stretching his wings in preparation. Tay turned to me and put my arms around his neck. "Just try to keep yourself afloat. Don't let go." His eyes were intense. I nodded, praying that he wouldn't let me drown.

"Okay," he said, guiding me towards the edge of the boat. "On three, we all jump."

Oh God.

"One."

How deep is that water?

"Two."

I don't want to die.

"Three!"

"I'm not ready!" I screamed my last thought aloud, but it was no use. Taylor jumped into the air and Tay plunged into the sea, dragging me along with him. For a moment we were under water, the ocean frigid and dark, but Tay quickly pulled me to the surface. I clung to him for dear life as he fixed our life jackets and paddled towards land. I was shivering and gasping for breath as Taylor flew alongside us.

We continued on like that for a while, my panic receding as the city grew closer. I tried my best to keep my head high above the water, terrified of what monsters I might see swimming below us if I dared look down. Tay stopped swimming for a moment, treading water and letting our life jackets keep us afloat. "I'm getting tired. We're going to let to waves push us to shore for a while." I didn't want to stay in the water for any long than we had to, but I didn't want Tay to drown from exhaustion, either.

The waves did move us forward, but they did so at an excruciatingly slow pace. Taylor was having trouble staying in the air, and he gently lowered himself into the sea, clinging to Tay with one arm and holding the mug high above his head with the other. And so we floated there in the ocean, my clothes and hair absorbing uncomfortably cold amounts of water and my mouth and nose stinging from salt, waiting for Tay to gain back enough strength to bring us the rest of the way to shore.

After another ten minutes or so, Tay started swimming, but he stopped abruptly. "Oh, dear god..." he whispered.

"What? What is it?" I asked, panicking more than just a little.

All that Tay could bring himself to do was point. Below and a little in front of us, maybe twenty feet under the water, was a cluster of tentacles. They were like that of a squid, but longer and thicker than those of any squid I'd ever seen, and they were rising out of the water. Suddenly, not ten feet in front of us, a fifty-foot-tall giant squid monster rocketed to the surface of the sea. We stared at the massive beast in horror; it was too big to swim around quickly, and even if we could, we had no idea if it would try and chase us or not. Or grab us in its tentacles, or try to eat us, or drag us under the water...

The squid looked down at us with its gargantuan green eyes, as if contemplating how it would kill us. Slowly, carefully, Tay gently paddled to the left, trying to steer us away from the monster. It didn't move, but it followed us with its eyes. Suddenly, it began to screech, an awful, high-pitched call. An oddly familiar call. A loud and unwavering "SCREEEEEEEEEE!!!"

"Mothman!" I cried in excitement. The squid wasn't making any noise at all; our mothy friend was. He flew over the squid's head and hovered over us, flying in excited little circles and making excited little screeches, as if trying to say *I found you! I found you!*

"We're so happy to see you!" Taylor cried. "Can you get us out of here?"

Mothman lifted us in his arms one by one, shifting Taylor to his back and carrying me and Tay in either arm. He soared into the sky. The giant squid sluggishly raised a tentacle and swatted at us as we passed, but Mothman dodged it with ease. The squid turned to watch us go, and then sank back under the water. In less than a minute, Mothman dropped us off near a big black Sudan. In front of it stood Drake himself, his hair frazzled and awry, a pair of black binoculars around his neck, and a long black overcoat running from his shoulders to his ankles.

"Children," he said, spreading his arms in a welcoming gesture. "I'm glad you could make it." It was strange to see him again after just talking to him on the phone for so long. He looked like he had aged a great deal in the week since we'd first met him.

"It's good to see you" Taylor said, "but what are you doing here? And how did Mothman find us? We didn't summon him yet."

Any semblance of joy in Drake's face quickly evaporated. "I'll answer the easier question first," he said, "Mothman has an excellent sense of smell, as you know. I gave him the T-shirt you sent Mercy's skull back in, and much like a bloodhound, Mothman tracked down your hotel room, where I picked up your bags and your cat. When you didn't answer my phone calls, he tracked down you three as well. It looks like it was a good thing, too. You three seemed like you were in a great deal of trouble." No one had noticed the ringing phone; he was probably calling us during our fight with Bernard Coy, when we'd all been too busy fighting for our lives to pay even the slightest attention to anything else.

"Meow!" Spooky popped up from behind the driver's seat window, and Drake opened the door to let him out. He jumped down from the seat and bolted over to Tay, Taylor, and me, rubbing himself around all our feet and purring.

"Oh, Spooky!" I said, picking him up and holding my precious kitty. "I'm so happy we didn't take you on that boat!"

"You were right, he is a strange-looking feline, but he's definitely a real cat," Drake said with a smile. "He makes a good pet. He sat on my lap the whole drive here."

I was overjoyed that Spooky was safe, but Drake wouldn't have come out to get him for us if something wasn't wrong.

"Drake, why are you here?" I asked. His smile disappeared once more and he let out a deep sigh.

"Children, I've gotten word that Conan is in the area."

"Okay," Tay said slowly, "we've dealt with him before. We can do it again."

"I'm afraid it's going to be different this time," Drake said, "I can't just send you away from him again. He's gotten enough universal objects. He's going to try and send us into the layer of the Unreal tonight." He looked each of us in the eyes. "We're going to have to face him head-on. I came to you because I'm going to need your help."

CONAN

We sat in the back of Drake's black Sudan while he drove down the streets of San Francisco. Mothman sat in the front seat beside him, and Spooky was curled up on Taylor's lap.

Drake gave us a rundown of what was going to happen. Conan had a secret hideout in the Redwood forest. Two other trios were in close enough proximity that Drake hoped they could join us there (one of which was the trio that had discovered the hideout; Drake used them exclusively for spying). The plan was to ambush Conan before we could harness the powers of his objects, take them for our own use, and somehow convince Conan to give us the spell needed to get back to the real layer. The best case scenario was that everything would somehow go perfectly and we could all get to go home tonight. An okay case scenario was that Conan would escape without giving us the spell, but we would prevent Conan from sending us into the Unreal. The worst case scenario was that Conan would succeed and we would fail. It was hard to imagine that for better or worse, everything could very well be over tonight. I had expected to be in this layer much longer than a week, and yet it was all coming to an end so soon. I was nervous; I didn't want to fail and let Conan win. I didn't want to face him.

I dug my jacket out of my backpack and put it on. Drake had given us a few small washcloths to dry off with – it was all he had with him – but they didn't work very well and I was still cold from the ocean. I offered to take the cellphone from Tay and keep it in my pocket – he was carrying it in his hand because his pockets were still soaking wet – and he gratefully accepted. I dug around in my backpack some more and pulled out two more important things- the drawing of us that Taylor had made, and Conan's music box. The time to use the music box would be soon, and the drawing gave me a sense of comfort, even if it was only a little.

I thought about all the ways tonight could end up. If we didn't stop Conan but we didn't go to the layer of the Unreal, how much longer would we be here? If we did go to the Unreal, what would happen? Drake seemed to think there was a high chance we would die instantly. Maybe we'd get there all right, but then be killed by all the extra monsters and demons that roamed the layer. Drake didn't think we could ever get back home from that layer, so even if we survived, life in the Unreal wouldn't be worth living.

I thought about what it would be like if I did get to go home. I wasn't ready to go to Providence with my cousin, but then again, would I ever be? And how would she react to seeing me after I had gone missing for a week? How could I ever explain what had happened to me? I couldn't possibly make up a convincing enough lie, but if I told the truth, no one would ever believe me.

I thought about Tay and Taylor, too. What would happen to our friendship – to *us*? I knew in my heart that I didn't want to lose them. We hadn't known each other for very long, but we'd built a strong relationship in the past week; we'd done things together that we'd never do with anyone else, shared experiences that were indescribable, once in a lifetime events. Our bond was new, but incredibly special. If I could help it, I wasn't letting them go.

I knew I probably wouldn't be able to see them much in the next three years because we were all still kids and we lived thousands of miles away from each other, but we could email and talk on the phone. And once we graduated high school, we could see each other more often. Maybe I could find a nursing school in San Francisco and Taylor could move out there to paint. Tay could wander the streets playing guitar like he wanted to. I'd let him sleep in my dorm at night whenever he needed it, and Taylor could stay with me, too. Or maybe Taylor and I could get part-time jobs and together with Tay's performance money we could get an apartment together and just live there. And we'd adopt

Spooky and he'd live with us, too, and Drake and Mothman could visit for holidays and birthdays or just whenever they were in town.

It sounded heavenly – living with my two best friends, each of us following our dreams in the most beautiful city in the world, with a cat and a moth and a genius to keep us company. It was strange, but the dream made me angry. It made me angrier at Conan, more determined than ever to take him down. In that moment, I wanted my happy ending, no matter what it took.

Drake turned down the classic rock that had been playing on the radio and glanced at us in the rear view mirror.

"Children, I'm curious and I forgot to ask," he said, "what happened to you on Alcatraz? I thought there were regular ferries to and from the island; why were you in the ocean?"

Tay explained to him everything that had happened, from Bernard Coy sauntering out of the jail and later onto the boat, to our seemingly impossible fist-fight, to our boat sinking under the water. Drake was silent for a while after he finished, his expression stoic in the rearview mirror.

"The fact that you could touch him, that he could leave the island..." he started. "That isn't good. It means we're slipping farther from the real layer and becoming more deeply ingrained with this one. It means that even if we stop Conan from moving us to the Unreal tonight, he's at least very close to moving us back another layer. Almost certainly even *more* than one layer. Children, we... this..." He took a deep breath, choosing his words carefully. "Let's just hope this ends tonight."

As Drake drove and time passed, we went from city to suburbs, from suburbs to farmland, and from farmland to forest. We were in an endless forest of Redwoods, which I had always known were the biggest trees on earth but had never realized that the word "big" didn't quite cut it. The Christmas tree in town square was big. The oak trees by my church were big. These trees were so much larger than that; over three hundred feet tall and counting, as tall as the Statue of Liberty and wider than four people together could fit their arms around. They were a nice distraction from our upcoming battle, but they were also a grave reminder that we were only getting closer to it.

Drake pulled into a small clearing in the trees, just off the road. It looked like a sort of parking lot for some hiking trails. There was only one other car there, a blue minivan with three stocky women in their mid-thirties leaning against it, and to my surprise, when we pulled into a spot near them they waved and approached the car. They were from our layer; a trio like us working for Drake.

"Time to get out of the car," Drake told us, leaning over to unbuckle Mothman's seatbelt. "You must introduce yourselves."

Mothman leapt out of the car first, running up to the women with an excited "SCRRREEEEEEEEEE!!!" and enveloping all three of them in a bear hug.

"Aw, we missed ya too, buddy," one of them said.

Drake cleared his throat, and the women wriggled out from Mothman's embrace and turned to face us. I hovered a bit behind Tay and Taylor, feeling shy again.

"Children, these women are all named Christina, but they go by their middle names," Drake told us. "This is Rachel." The woman on the left waved. She had the same wavy brown hair and stocky build that the other Christinas did, but she was shorter, with a freckled, friendly face.

"This is Marie." Drake gestured to the woman in the middle, who had bright blue eyes as opposed to the brown eyes of the other two.

"And this is Esther." Esther was the biggest of the three, with bulging biceps and a hard, stoic face.

"And these children are all named Taylor," Drake said, gesturing to us. "But they go by Tay, Lori, and Taylor."

We said a few more awkward hellos and then Drake cleared his throat. He pointed to a small log cabin in the distance. It looked abandoned and in an awful state of disrepair, like it hadn't been used in years. "Children, over there is Conan's hideout. It looks unused, but the basement is large and quite advanced."

"We think there's some traps around there, Drake," Esther said, "we disabled the bear traps we found, but we don't know what else is out there."

"I'll bet he's got some monsters guarding it too," Marie chimed in.

"I wouldn't be surprised," Drake said, "Conan isn't stupid. He must have some worries about being found." The three women nodded in agreement.

"Are the Jacobs joining us?" asked Rachel.

Drake sighed. "I'm not sure. They're trying, but I can't tell if they'll make it in time. We can't wait for them much longer; the more time we spend out here, the more time Conan has to find out about us. Let's get out the weapons.

Marie turned around and popped open the trunk of the minivan. My jaw dropped open. Inside was a miniature weaponry, complete with machine guns, handguns, hunting rifles, a flamethrower, and blades ranging in size from machetes to Swiss army knives. Marie took three of the biggest guns.

"An M-16 for you," she said to Rachel, handing her the weapon. "An assault rifle for me, and an Uzi for Esther." Esther took her gun with a huge smile. Marie then handed a smaller pistol to Drake, who tucked it into one of the pockets of his overcoat.

"You kids know how to shoot?" she hollered. I looked to Tay and Taylor. They looked just as overwhelmed as I was, and we all shook our heads.

"They were in a fistfight with a dead man today and have battled canine monsters in the past, but that's it. They've only been here a week," Drake told her.

"Give 'em some hunting knifes. Medium length," instructed Esther. Marie complied, and soon I was holding a five-inch-long silver blade in my hand. I swallowed hard, hoping no one would be bothered by the fact that I had absolutely no idea how to use it. Grandma would have grounded me for months and taken away all my books if she had caught me with such a weapon back home. This all felt so out of place.

"Screeee?" cried Mothman curiously, reaching for the flamethrower. Rachel quickly reached over and shut the trunk.

"No, buddy, you fight well enough without a weapon. You remember what happened last time," she chided.

Mothman wrung his hands. "Screeeee," he confirmed.

"Alright," Drake said, looking at the cabin behind us. "Are we ready to get started? It might take us a while to get inside."

"So this is it? We're just... charging?" Tay asked. It was the first time I'd heard him speak in hours. We were silent almost the entire car ride.

Drake nodded. "We'll fight our way to Conan the way you have been fighting for special objects all this time: by playing it by ear and making strategies as we go along. If it's a monster, we shoot. If it's a puzzle or trap, we'll use our minds. There's no one clear way to win this because we don't know what awaits us, but we'll fight it the best that we can. Just like you always have."

Drake's words somehow comforted me. He was right, this was no different than everything else we'd done this week, just a bigger and more complicated version. Like each location we went to was a unit test, and this cabin was the semester final. It was big and scary at first, but if you broke it down, it was manageable.

Esther patted down her pants pockets and frowned. "You know what, Drake? I left some extra ammo in the truck. I'll go get it."

She turned and started walking back to the car. Marie looked to the knife in Taylor's grip. "You're holding it wrong," she said, "I'll show you how to use it while we wait for Esther to get back."

Rachel took Tay's knife and started giving him some pointers, and Drake tried to explain the same basic principles to me. As he leaned over to fix my grip, his pistol fell out from his overcoat. He grunted and bent over to pick it up, but the moment he touched the weapon the scene around me changed.

I saw Drake standing on a beach, the ocean in front of him and a towering rocky cliff to his back. Sheets of rain poured from a misty grey sky. Two men, brunet and pale, were on the beach with Drake;

otherwise, the group was completely isolated. One man lay broken and bloody on the sand while the other kneeled over him. Drake stood at the kneeling man's shoulder, emotionless.

"We need to keep moving," Drake commanded.

"I told you, I'm not leaving him!" The man shot back. "He's still breathing."

"He's not going to get any better, James! We can't move him!" Drake knelt down and put a hand on James's shoulder. "Remember what I told you? I can fix this. I work for the government and I study paranormal occurrences. I have a lab back in Nevada. If I could just—"

"Then GO, Drake! Leave!"

"You know that's not possible if you two don't come with me!" Drake roared. Slowly, he drew a pistol from his pocket. James froze.

"We'll put him out of his misery. Then we can go." Drake explained.

"NO!" cried James. He grabbed the bloody man under his shoulders and tried hoisting him up, tried dragging him away. He was barely able to move the man two inches before he gave up and dropped him, panting. He erupted in tears.

"I won't leave him," he repeated.

James sobbed over the body, his back to Drake. Drake slipped the pistol out of his pocket and turned off the safety. *He needed to get to Area 51. He knew he could fix everything.*

He wrapped his finger around the trigger.

He pointed the weapon at James.

He pulled the trigger.

I jerked out of the memory with a gasp. Drake was staring at me, his dark eyes concerned. He reached out to touch my arm, but I pulled away. "Lori, are you alright?"

Conan was right. He'd done it. He'd killed them.

I eyed the gun in his hand and whispered, "Is that the same one you killed your trio with?"

Drake narrowed his eyes. "Who told—"

"It doesn't matter. I know." I snapped. A shiver ran down my spine. "How could you do something like that? How could you kill someone so connected to you?"

He sighed. "I knew I could find a way out of the Unreal if I could get back to my office. I also knew I couldn't do that if they were with me," Drake paused for a moment, a distant longing forming in his eyes.

"It's something I wish I hadn't had to do. I feel remorse for ending the lives of two good men, Lori, I feel it every single day. But you have to understand that no one would be here if I hadn't gotten back to Nevada. You and your trio would still be wandering the desert as would so many others."

Drake was right, I knew he was. I knew he was doing his best to help me. But I still felt so filthy to be standing so close to a murderer.

"I know, I just… It sounds so heartless. Like something Conan would do. I thought we were the good guys."

Drake's mouth shrunk into a tight, thin line.

"Lori, I want you to understand something. There is no 'good' and 'evil' in war. There is only our cause and theirs. If you find my actions morally objectionable, you don't have to fight with me. But this is the side of the war that will bring you home. I believe that is the cause you are looking to support."

"Is everyone ready now?" called Rachel.

Drake and I locked eyes, and he offered me his hand. Slowly, I reached over and shook it. Drake had made a mistake, a terrible, cruel mistake, but that didn't make him evil. And I needed him to help me go home.

I walked over to Tay and Taylor. I sheathed my knife, slipped it into my coat pocket, and took their hands. They both looked at me. *"We're okay,"* I whispered. Taylor smiled and looked towards the cabin. Tay squeezed my hand tighter.

"We're ready," I said. Drake nodded and turned away, facing the dilapidated cabin.

"Okay, then," he said, and he began the journey towards it. The Christinas fell in line behind him, and we followed them, still holding hands, with Mothman behind us. "Let's pray this works to our benefit," Drake whispered. We followed him deeper into the woods.

We were able to make it to the ruined front porch of the cabin with nothing happening to us. No monsters jumped out from behind a tree, no traps sprung up around our feet, no one was struck dead by a phantom bolt of lightning. We gathered ourselves around the blackened front door, studying it with caution. Was this really going to be so easy?

Drake put his hand on the door knob, then turned to face the rest of us. *Ready?* he mouthed. We all nodded, wielding our weapons in case something unwanted came out to meet us. *One*, mouthed Drake, holding up a finger, *Two, Three!*

Drake yanked open the door and flung himself out of the way. A dark shadow appeared in the door way, but before I could react, a barrage of gunfire assaulted my ears. All three Christinas showered bullets at the creature for a good five seconds, using what must have been several dozens of bullets. If whatever was in the doorway was killable, there was no way it wasn't dead.

The shadow paused for a moment after the gunfire ceased, and then drifted further out the door. We all gasped and took a step back, preparing to defend ourselves against whatever dared come out of that door.

A black, misty ghost emerged from the doorway and hovered about two feet above the front porch. The face of the ghost was that of an old man, an old man with a burned face, a gaping mouth, and bloodshot eyes. He stared at us for a moment, then evaporated into the air. The eight us of us were silent for a moment, regaining our composure. Then, Drake pulled back the door again, peering into the room behind it.

"It looks safe," he said, gesturing for us to come in. He slowly made his way into the room, and we nervously followed. I was desperately hoping for no more ghostly surprises.

The room was fairly dark, the only light coming from two small windows on the left and right walls and from a tiny hole in the falling-apart roof. It was mostly empty, with only a simple wooden table in the center of the floor and a rolled-up rug in one corner. It seemed harmless enough – definitely creepy, but no more so than any other abandoned building – until Drake led us to a far corner.

On the lower wall was a massive pentagram, drawn using a red substance that looked suspiciously like blood. In front of it sat an Ouija board accompanied by a skull with a candle melted on top of it. The corner was definitely satanic, the kind of thing I had been warned to stay away from by my Grandma and my pastors for almost all my life. I didn't want to go near it, but Drake put his hands on the little wooden planchette and gestured for us to join him. "I need one Christina and one Taylor for this to work," he said. "Marie, did you figure out the passcode?"

"Yes," Marie said, "it's the name Vanessa and the name Isaac. The family he lost." Marie kneeled over the board and with Drake, and Tay reluctantly broke away from us to join them. I clung to Taylor and Mothman, unsure of but anxious for what was going to happen.

Drake, Marie, and Tay slowly moved the planchette over the proper letters of the board, spelling out V-A-N-E-S-S-A and then I-S-A-A-C. As soon as they finished, the wall above us began to rumble. The pentagram twisted in the wall and then swung out, opening up a circular door in the wall. Drake peered down the hole and motioned for us to follow him. We squeezed ourselves through the child-sized passage and soon stood on the top of a long spiral staircase, with more skull-candles lining the walls. But this time, they were lit, creating an eerie orange-ish glow against the brown oak paneling and staircase of the room. I peeked over the railing, but I couldn't tell where the stairs ended; they seemed to go on forever.

After getting the all clear signal from Drake, we cautiously began out journey down the never-ending spiral of stairs into the dark world below.

The walk down the stairs seemed to take an eternity, but I couldn't tell if it was due to their incredible length or my own impending sense of doom.

Finally, we reached a steel door at the bottom of the stairway, emblazoned with the face of a fanged wolf. Drake put his hand on the handle and twisted. It turned with his hand, but he let it go instead of opening the door.

"It's unlocked," he said. He turned to face the rest of us, his face serious. "I can't be sure, but Conan could very well be behind this door."

I swallowed hard, holding Tay's and Taylor's hands tighter and checking to make sure that Mothman was still behind me. My heart was beating faster than I had previously thought possible; was this it? Were we going to fight him now? I wasn't ready, but then again, would I ever be?

"Remember, we don't want to kill him right away," Drake said. "Be careful with the guns. We can't get back to our layer using his objects alone, we need the spell, too, which only he knows. And if he's dead, we may never be able to get it." We all nodded in understanding, and Esther took her finger off the trigger of her Uzi. Drake took a deep breath and put his hand back on the door knob.

"One," he said.

I squeezed Tay and Taylor's hands tighter still.

"Two."

I shut my eyes, but then opened them again. This wasn't a roller coaster or a scary movie. I couldn't just look away until the worst was over.

"Three!" Drake ripped open the door and we bolted into the room, guns, knives, and claws ready.

The room was huge, with ceilings at least forty or fifty feet in the air and enough space to make up a high school cafeteria. The floor was a steely metallic silver and the walls and ceiling were a pitch black.

And there, in the center of the room, leaning over a lab table, stood Conan, his eyes wide with shock upon seeing us. He whipped a pistol of his own from his pocket and pointed it in our direction, moving the barrel from Drake to Taylor to Rachel to Mothman to Drake again as he tried to figure out who was the biggest threat to him. "Do. Not. Move," he commanded.

"We want that spell, Conan," Drake said, his voice booming in the massive, echoing room. "Just give it to us and no one will get hurt."

"And how do I know I can trust you?" Conan retorted, steadying his grip on the pistol, which he now very confidently aimed at Drake. "You burst into my lab with all those big weapons; surely you're up to no good."

"Enough, Conan. Give us the objects and the spell. It's eight against one. You're overpowered."

Conan raised his human eyebrow, his mouth twisting into a strange smile. "Oh, am I now?" He backed away, into the darkness of the far side of the room. "That's funny you should say that, really, because it simply isn't true. I think it's you who is overpowered, Drake."

I looked to Tay and Taylor and the Christinas, who seemed just as confused and terror-struck as I was. Dear lord, what was he hiding?

Conan saw the panic on our faces and smiled. "You didn't *really* think I'd be in here all alone, did you?" he asked, his tone condescending and dripping with mock sympathy.

He threw his head to the sky and howled. He smiled at us, his expression smug and joyous. A second howl sounded in the distance. Then a third. Then a fourth.

I looked up and realized there was a small metal stairway in the back of the room that lead up to metal walkways lining the upper walls of the room, like the second floor of the Museum of Natural History or the catwalks of a theater. Appearing at their railings from every direction were hundreds of huge monster-wolves, the very same kind we had battled in Washington DC.

Next, the sound of a garage door opening rumbled from the far wall, the one behind Conan. The oversized door on the wall rose to the ceiling, revealing a black crevice behind it. A strange kind of growling emitted from the tunnel, implying that there was an even bigger monster waiting for us behind it. Conan smiled and continued to back away.

"I do hope you'll enjoy playing with my friends," he said. "They've been lonely." And with that, he howled once more. The wolves jumped from their positions on the walkways, pouring out onto the floor around us while Conan sprinted away.

"Don't let him get away!" Drake cried with fury, ignoring the monsters and bolting in Conan's direction, but a blood curdling screech cut him off.

Emerging from the garage door was a monster bigger than an elephant, with a green, scaly, dinosaur-like body and five long necks. The heads were snake-like, with wide mouths, red eyes, and giant pointed teeth. I recognized it from my childhood book of Greek Mythology: a hydra. For every head we cut off, two more would grow back.

A sudden rain of gunfire rang out from either side of me as Esther and Rachel mowed down the incoming wolves, slaughtering them like they were nothing more than harmless bunny rabbits. A few of them were avoiding the rain of bullets, however, and one jumped over Esther's head and tried to pounce on Taylor, only to be deflected by a stab to the ribs from Tay's knife and the claws and jaws of a furious Mothman.

I heard a furious yowl somewhere behind me, and I spun around, preparing to defend myself against another wolf, only to see my little Spooky rushing onto the battlefield. He leapt into the air, soaring over my head and into the mass of oncoming monsters, but as he did so, he suddenly wasn't a little hairless cat anymore. He completely transformed into a growling, muscular saber-toothed tiger in mid-air. When he hit the ground, it shook from the force of his weight. He barred his teeth and roared, a booming battle cry that sent several wolves running with their tails between their legs.

A great gray wolf launched itself off Spooky's back and tried to pounce on my trio and I, but we intercepted it with our knives. I took a stab at the wolf's back and instantly regretted it. The feeling of jabbing a knife into another living being's flesh was sickening, and the sound that came with me removing the knife to use it again was even worse.

I can't be out here. This isn't how I fight, I thought as Mothman dug his claws into yet another wolf and hurled it into the wall. How had I gotten through all our other conflicts in this reality? I remembered Annabelle, where I had grabbed the doll and dashed out the door despite Tay's protests and fears. I remembered Mercy, where I had calmed down a furious spirit just by listening to her. The only reason we were able to get the cross from the imp at the City Museum was because I had enlisted Winnie's help, and Sarah Winchester had told me how to find her bedsheets. My successes in this layer hadn't come by taking things by force or killing every danger I came across; they had come from deep thinking, patience, and kindness. *You have a gift, Lori, a gift that is unique among both your friends and your enemies.* I had Conan's music box in my pocket. I could stop him. I could stop him if only I could get to that staircase.

I looked around. Esther and Rachel were being more conservative with their bullets so they didn't run out, but the wolves' numbers were quickly diminishing, and Tay, Taylor, and Mothman were easily picking up the slack. Drake and Marie were futilely firing bullets at the Hydra, but they couldn't pierce the beast's thick, scale-covered hide. However, the Hydra was trying to bite them with one of its many heads, and it seemed like it was struggling almost more than they were. Every time it brought one of its heads within striking range, Marie or Drake would wham the back of their guns into the creature's skull, causing it to roar in pain and anger. They weren't winning the battle against it, but they were holding it off pretty well, and surely enough wolves would die that they could get back up from the others in time.

I ran my eyes along the back of the room, scoping out a path to the staircase Conan had run up. The hydra was blocking it, but I had an idea. It was now or never.

"I'll be back! Stay here; I'll be done in no time!" I called to Tay and Taylor, practically screaming to be heard over all the noise.

"Wait, what?!" Taylor cried.

"Where the hell are you going?" Tay yelled, as he fended off a snarling silver wolf with a sharp jab to its face.

Now! I thought, seeing the pathway totally clear of wolves I took off running, calling over my shoulder, "Don't worry! Love you!"

I bolted to the hydra faster than I'd ever run in my life and dashed underneath its chest, running straight between Drake and Marie and in between the beast's legs, thankful that no wolves had followed me. I rocketed up the stairs and looked around the hallways; more wolves were emerging and jumping to the floor from the left and right sides, but not nearly as many as there had been initially.

I saw another hallway; a proper hallway that actually went into the wall, to my left, and ran for it, hoping it was the way that Conan had escaped. As I dashed down it, I noticed a series of doors on either side of me; wooden doors with a window at the top, like the doors you see in schools. Behind each door was another science lab, with random assumedly universal objects scattered around the tables. I reached the end of the hall with no sign of Conan and took a break, panting. I hadn't seen another hallway like this one, but I supposed I could look again. I turned around and started running again only to ram straight into something and fall to the floor.

I pushed myself off the ground and looked up; there, on the floor in from of me, was Conan. We stared at each other in shock for a moment, his brown and green eyes wide with panic, and then he pulled out his gun. Instinctively, I pulled out my knife, but I soon realized it would be useless against Conan's weapon. I had literally brought a knife to a gunfight.

Conan pointed the weapon at me for a moment, his hands shaking, but before I had time to react he sprung to his feet and bolted down the hall.

"HEY!" I called, chasing after him. He ran back across the catwalk and turned to the left, running towards the back of the room.

He yanked open a camouflaged black door at the end of the catwalk and jumped inside. The new hallway was lightless and unknown to me, but I knew I had to follow him. I ran as fast as I could through the darkness, hoping that if I ran fast enough no monster would be able to leap out of the halls and attack me.

Yet another set of metal spiral stairs rested at the end of the hallway, and Conan thundered up them. I copied him, chasing him from below. He fired his gun at my feet as he ran, trying to stop me from going any higher. But his aim was shaky and his bullets always missed, and I never stopped climbing the long, winding staircase.

Finally, I reached the top of the stairs and was met by Conan, standing alone in a small room with shelves upon shelves of universal objects. He pointed his gun at me again, his hands shaking out of control.

"D-do not! Come any closer!" he whimpered, his voice like that of a child trying not to cry. I lingered in the doorway, silently obeying his orders. Slowly, I lowered my knife.

"I don't want to hurt you," I said, "I just want to talk."

"I can't give you that spell!" he yelled. "I can't quit now! I'm not about to lose them, no matter what you do!"

I suddenly understood his resistance, his endless tricks he had up his sleeve.

There is no 'good' and 'evil' in war. There is only our cause and theirs.

I hadn't considered tonight from Conan's point of view. If he won, he would hopefully survive the journey to the Unreal and be able to find his family again. If he lost, he would be back at square one, back to his old, miserable life without anyone. Somehow, I was going to have to convince him that life at this square one was still a life worth living; not only that he didn't need to bring back the dead, but that he just plain *shouldn't* bring back the dead. I needed to convince him that all the destruction he was causing wasn't worth it. If I truly had a "gift," now was the time to use it. I didn't know how I could, but I needed to trust my ability to talk, to listen, to empathize.

"I understand," I said, "you don't want to start over again. You don't want to lose them. But, Conan," I stepped towards him now, but he raised his gun again, so I stopped. "Have you considered that maybe they don't want to be found?"

The beast-faced man threw back his head in laughter. "Trying to talk me down, are you? We've been through this. Your grandmother died of old age. She got to live. My family never had that chance."

"I know, I know," I said, "but look at yourself. Look at your face. Look at the world you've created. It's full of death and destruction. Is that what Isaac and Vanessa wanted? For you to become a murderer?" His face turned venomous at my words.

"The end justifies the means, Lori," he said, his voice low and his face dark. "This isn't the perfect way, but it's the only way. I need to see them again."

"But you *will* see them again. You know that afterlives exist in the Unreal now, if you just believe in the same one they did then—"

"They didn't have a religion!" he howled at me, his face red with fury. "I don't know where they are! What afterlife they went to, if they even went to one at all! I can't trust that I'll end up in the same place they did!" He took a deep breath, lowering his gun. "There's too much uncertainty in death." He looked me right in the eyes, his fury replaced with sadness, longing, and exhaustion. "I have to find them this way. I'm sorry for all the pain it's caused. But I have to find them this way or I won't be able to find them at all."

He sank down to the floor now, cross legged, his gun lowered but still clutched tightly in his left hand.

"You miss them," I said quietly. He sighed, sounding tired and annoyed.

"Yes, Lori," he said, as if explaining something trivial to a child, "I miss them very much."

The Conan on the floor in front of me faded away and was replaced with a vision of a smaller, younger Conan sitting on a playground. His face was fully human, but his eyes were still different colors. The boy was wearing a too-big, falling-apart T-shirt and was in desperate need of a good haircut. He sat behind a tiny blue backpack, far away from the swings and slides that the other children played on. Slowly, cautiously, he removed a pair of knitting needles and a halfway finished scarf from the bag. He knit with a deliberate lack of speed, a careful attention to detail. He was completely engrossed in making the scarf.

He was so engrossed in making the scarf that he didn't notice the two older boys marching towards him until the needles were shoved out of his hands.

"You're a prissy."

Conan refused to look up at his tormenters. He picked the needles and yarn off the ground and restarted the project right where he had left off. The scarf and needles were slammed out of his hands yet again.

"A pansy."

The situation repeated itself, with Conan seemingly hoping that the problem would disappear if only he ignored it.

The clatter of metal needles on cement.

"An embarrassment."

Conan did his best to continue his scarf no matter how many times it was torn away from him. He never said a word, but he couldn't blink back all of the tears that were swelling beneath his eyes.

One boy turned to the other, snickering. "See? It's so easy to make this kid cry." He put his hand on the scarf. "You're a—"

"SHUT UP!" At first, I thought the yell had come from Conan, but he still sat silently staring at his knitting. A teenaged boy was storming towards the bullies. He looked like Conan, the same hair color and facial features, but both his eyes were brown.

Both boys took off running.

The teenager squatted beside Conan. "Did they hurt you?"

For the first time, young Conan spoke. "No," he whispered.

He finally looked up from the scarf and needles and into the teen's eyes. He held up his now dirty, frizzy project. "But they…"

The teen groaned, took the project and tossed it into Conan's little backpack and zipped it up for him. "Conan, you've got to start standing up for yourself. What are you gonna do when I start high school next year, huh?"

The teen helped Conan put the bag over his shoulders and took his hand. The two walked away from the playground together.

"You'll still be my brother. You can still protect me."

Conan's brother, he must have been Isaac, sighed. "Not until four o'clock, I won't be able to." He stopped walking. "Look Conan, I'm always going to be there for you. But you need someone else in your life, too. Someone your age. Someone who's like you."

Conan looked away. "I can't make any friends. No one's like me."

Isaac smiled at his brother and started walking with him again. "Do you remember my friend Alex?"

"Yeah."

"Well, I just met his cousin. She's your age, and she goes to school at St. Mark's. She loves sewing and ghost stories and musicals too. I asked her to come to our house this afternoon so you could meet her."

Conan stopped mid-step in the middle of the sidewalk.

"Isaac, no!"

"She won't be mean, Conan, I promise. I just want you to see her." Isaac squeezed his brother's hand and looked into his mismatched eyes. "She's just like you."

Little Conan found reassurance in his brother's words, and the two finished the walk and arrived at a small, one story home with a yellow door and falling-apart shingles. Isaac smiled at Conan one last time before unlocking the door and ushering his brother inside.

A cute little black girl with her hair in two braids sat at the counter, her face buried in a book. Issac clapped his brother on the shoulder. "Conan, I want you to meet Vanessa. Vanessa, this is Conan."

The girl lifted her face from her book with a smile and met Conan's eyes. As soon as she did, they both gasped.

One of her irises was brown.

The other was green.

The vision of young Conan evaporated, and I was left staring at the man that once-innocent child had become. *Yes, Lori, I miss them very much.*

"I know what that feels like," I said, approaching him slowly. He watched me with caution, but he did not raise his gun. "I miss my grandma. She protected and loved me too. And my heart breaks for her every day she's gone. But I just can't go find—"

Suddenly Conan was back on his feet and yelling.

"You don't know what it's like! You didn't love her like I loved—"

"I DID!" I cried, cutting him off. I was surprised at myself; I hadn't planned to say that. But I didn't regret it, the words felt right, they were the truth. "I *did* love her like that," I whispered.

"Really?" Conan said. "If you really loved her, then how are you going to live without her? How will you be happy, how will you be fulfilled and content with your life and feel like nothing is missing and not wake up with a hole in your heart ever morning and feel nothing but emptiness inside and—"

I surprised myself again when I felt a frog in my throat and hot water behind my eyes. My sobs cut Conan off.

"I don't know," I said weakly, "I don't know how I'm going to live without her." Conan stood above me, watching me cry with cold, expressionless eyes. "I-I'm going to have to move in with my cousin in Providence," I babbled on. I didn't know why I was telling him this, because there was no way Conan cared. "I have to start life all over again. Everything's going to be different in the worst way. I don't know how I'm going to make it."

I had an idea; a way I could use my gift. I didn't know if it would work, but I had to try. I brought a memory to the forefront of my mind and used all my mental will power to direct it to Conan.

The scene playing out before us faded, and Conan and I stood side-by-side on Smart Street in Concord, New Hampshire, November 18, 2006. Together, we watched a small blonde girl riding her bike down the sidewalk. The sky was just beginning to darken, but she was only a few houses away from her own. She had very much been enjoying her evening ride until she realized that one of the neighbors had left their front gate open and their Rottweiler in the yard. It was a big dog, bigger than the small girl on the bike, and it was both ferocious and incredibly mean. The girl yelped upon seeing it and peddled faster, but the dog interpreted the scream and the fast bike as a challenge. It took off after her, chasing the still-screaming girl down the road. She peddled her little pink bike as fast as she possibly could, but when she threw her bike to the ground and bounded to her front door, she tugged at the handle to find it was locked. She turned to see the dog racing up her driveway and screamed bloody murder as the barking grew louder and the beast drew closer, its mouth full of snarling white fangs.

Suddenly another figure appeared in front of the girl like a shield, swatting at the dog's snout with a gardening hoe and yelling "Git! GIT!" She forced the dog's clenched jaws off the sleeve of her sweatshirt and sent it whimpering from the yard after a final bop to the nose, mostly unhurt but fearful.

The woman turned to the girl. Her hair was short and gray and curled, her face wrinkled but gentle. She was my grandma.

"Taylor!" she chided. "What did I tell you about leaving the yard after six? Especially without a coat!"

The girl looked down at her feet, ashamed. "Grandma, I'm sor—"

Before the child could finish her sentence she was wrapped in a hug from her grandmother. "Oh, I'm glad you're alright, sweetie. But promise me you'll never, *ever*, do something so absolutely silly again. Alright?"

The girl nodded. Her grandma took a set of keys out of her pocket and unlocked the front door. As she did this, her granddaughter noticed a huge tear in the sleeve of her blue Wellesley College sweatshirt. "Oh, Grandma…"

Grandma looked down at the rip little Taylor pointed to.

"Oh," she said, "oh, dear."

The girl bit her lip. "Was that the one Mom used to wear?"

Her grandma sighed. "Yes Taylor, it is."

The little girl hung her head and tried not to cry.

"I'm so sorry, Grandma! Can we fix—"

"Taylor." Grandma cut little her off. "I'm not mad at you for this. You're the only memento of your mother's that I need. That's why you have to stay safe, darling. I don't want to catch you breaking any more rules." She looked into her granddaughter's eyes, my eyes. "Okay?"

I smiled, both in the past and in the present.

"Okay."

I cut off the memory and let it fade away, forcing Conan and I back to reality. He looked at me and paused, blinking his eyes hard. He reached out and put a hand on my shoulder.

"Lori," he said, "help me. Go get your Grandmother. You don't have to live without her."

"But that isn't what she wanted!" I said. "She wanted me to grow up and live life and be a nurse like she was. And that's what I want, too. I need to honor her memory."

Conan looked at me like he had bitten a sour lemon. He turned away in disgust. "Fine. If that's how you want to grieve, then I won't stop you. But my family didn't want a legacy from me. They didn't want anything from me."

"Did they love you? Did they care if you were happy or not?"

Conan paused for a moment. "Of course, but, but this is different!"

I reached into my pocket, feeling around for the music box. "Conan, when Captain von Trapp's wife died, he moved on, didn't he? He met Maria and learned to love his kids again and he was happy. He stopped living in the past."

"What on Earth are you talking—"

I pulled the music box out of my pocket and he stopped mid-sentence, his mouth hanging open. "Where did you get that?" he whispered.

"The Winchester Mystery House. Sarah was taking care of it for you." I stood and placed the little box in his cold, calloused hands. He turned it over and gently ran his fingers over the inscription from Vanessa on the back, his face like Taylor's when he looked out the shuttle windows at the city of St. Louis: gentle and filled with memory and wonder.

Conan gingerly opened the little box. The song "Edelweiss" began to play, and the delicate glass flower spun in place. I could see the tears welling in his eyes as he stared, mesmerized, at his long lost music box, his treasured token of his fiancée's love.

He began to sing. *"Edelweiss, Edelweiss."* His voice was deep and heavy, but it was beautiful. He slowly walked towards the door of the room, watching his little box and singing along with the gentle piano melody. *"Small and white, clean and bright, you look happy to meet me."*

Somewhere, in the vast metallic hallways below us, the sounds of chaos and commotion were echoing closer, growing louder by the second. A sick feeling came to my stomach. Something was raging toward us. I somehow just knew something was about to happen. Something bad.

I let Conan keep walking.

He paused in the doorway and turned to face me as the song ended, tears now streaming down his face.

"Thank—"

BANG!

The sounds of gunshots and people shouting ricocheted through the air and a bloody hole appeared in Conan's chest. He looked down and studied it in shock, reaching his hand up to feel the wound. He put two fingers to the hole and them held them up, his hand shaking as he studied the crimson fluid on his fingers. He collapsed to the floor.

"Conan!" I cried, rushing over to him. Drake told us not to kill him. If he died and I couldn't get the spell from him...

I whipped off my jacket and tried to use it to stop the bleeding, but he grabbed my arm, his grip incredibly strong and forceful for a dying man.

"No," he whispered.

"Conan, please, you'll die!"

"I don't need to live anymore." He still cradled the music box in his right arm, clinging to it like a lifeline. He drew in a sharp breath and looked me right in the eyes. His gaze was intense; it seemed to pierce my very soul, and I couldn't look away.

"You... were right," he said. "They wouldn't want to see me like this." He let go of my arm and touched the chupacabra part of his face. "They wouldn't want to see me kill you."

He reached into a pocket on the inside of his cloak and took out a journal. He flipped through it at an agonizing snail-like pace, turning every page with renewed caution. He eventually found the page he was looking for, ripped it out, and handed it to me. On it were four different sets of instructions for four different spells. "That should be everything you'll need," he whispered, his voice raspy. He took another breath, and a well of blood rose up from the hole in his chest. "Go home, Lori."

I tried to press my jacket to his wound again, but he swatted at my arm, having none of it.

"Conan, you don't need to die so we can live. Come home with us. You can start a new life. You can learn to be happy again," I said.

He shook his head. "No. I know I can't search for my family in the Unreal. But I still can't live without them. This is for the best."

"Conan, you—"

"Shh!" he whispered. I knew I was going to have to respect his decision to die right then. It felt wrong, but I had the spells. I could go home, and that was all I needed. We had won, I should've be happy. But watching Conan die hurt me. He was a human; a strange, twisted, human, yes, but a human all the same. He had spent the past fifteen years of his life searching for his family instead of enjoying his time on earth; he had been robbed of a chance to live as much as his brother and fiancée had.

"Lori?" he asked, his voice barely audible. "Do you think I'm going to hell?"

"I... I couldn't say, I don't know how that's decided," I said, "but you've reformed. And you've always had good intentions." I looked down at his broken, bloody, wretched face. "If your family is out there, Conan, I know that you'll get to see them again. No god would be cruel enough to take that away from you."

Conan sighed, whispering, "I hope so, I hope so. I loved them very much." With a shaky hand, he held out his music box to me. "Crank the handle, will you?" he whispered. I wound up the music box and gingerly placed it back in his blood-soaked arms.

He watched the little flower as it turned along with the chords of the music, immune to the shouting and banging coming from the floor below us. He twisted his dying breaths into one last beautiful song. *"Edelweiss, Edelweiss, you, look happ-y to meet... me..."*

The tones of the music stopped abruptly, as wind-up music boxes often do, and Conan's song cut out just as quickly. I saw his glassy eyes and open mouth, and then I knew he was dead. I gently shut the music box and molded his still-warm hands around it, like a bride holding a bouquet of flowers. I shut his mouth and closed his eyes.

"Goodbye," I whispered, "I hope you find them."

I heard shouting and clanging and footsteps storming up metal, and soon Drake burst into the room, followed by Tay, Taylor, Rachel, Esther, Mothman, a normal sized, cat shaped Spooky, and who I assumed were three Jacobs who had made it after all.

"Lori!" Tay cried, his face brightening upon seeing me. "Lori, thank God, we thought you were dea—"

The last word caught in his throat as he saw bloody corpse of Conan in front of me.

Drake roared with fury at the sight of him. "I thought I told you all not to shoot him! I *know* I told you all not to shoot him!" He whirled around to yell at me. "Lori, what happened here?!"

"I don't know who shot him," I said, stepping forward. "But he gave me the spells."

A stunned silence fell over the room as I handed the piece of paper to Drake. He tore it from my hands and poured over the text, reading it like the front page of a newspaper advertising a disaster. We watched him read, waiting for his confirmation or denial, and the silence in the room was deafening. After a moment, Drake let out a series of gentle sobs, holding the paper to his chest.

"This is it. This will work," he cried. "We can go home."

No one moved for a moment, everyone stupefied from the sudden news. Then the reality of the announcement started to sink in. Rachel rushed forward, snatched the paper from his hands, studied it, and started to cry.

"This is really it," she sobbed, "I can see my daughter again."

Suddenly, the meaning of everyone's words hit me. *This is it, I can go home, I don't have to die.* I caught Tay's eyes from across the room, then Taylor's. I ran up and hugged them, both of them, as I cried. I could be a nurse like Grandma. I still had my best friends by my side. We didn't die. We made it.

I opened my eyes and peered over Tay's shoulder at his back, where there was a bloody handprint from where my hand had been. I suddenly remembered Conan, and turned back to look at his body, still coated in a maroon slick of blood and clutching to a now cherry-stained music box. Despite all my joy, my smile disappeared. My hands slipped from my friends' shoulders. I fell to the floor. The world went black.

GOODBYE

I woke up with something hard and warm beneath my back. As I opened my eyes, I was blinded by a bright light shining above me.

The sun.

I realized I was staring up at the sky. I was laying on asphalt. A big black Sudan was just to the left of me. I was in a parking lot. The parking lot outside of Conan's cabin, the one we had started in.

A strange hairless creature entered my vision. "Meow?" it said as it began pawing at my hair. It ran its rough, wet tongue over my nose. *Spooky!* I pushed myself up off the ground and lifted my little kitty into my arms, grateful that he was okay.

"Oh, buddy, thank goodness you aren't hurt!" I cried, kissing the top of his misshapen, hairless head. "I don't know how you did it, but thank you for coming to fight with us." He purred with affection but jumped out of my lap and ran away. I turned to watch him, wondering where he was running off to, and saw everyone, my Taylor and Tay, Drake and Mothman, and the Jacobs and the Christinas minus Marie, crowded around the bed of a big brown truck a good thirty feet behind me. A rush of memories came flooding back as I recalled the events up to my fainting spell.

We're free! I can go home! I slowly rose to my feet and cautiously made my way to the others, careful so that I wouldn't pass out again. As I inched closer to the group, I saw that they were studying a map of Nevada, with Drake pointing out roads and explaining directions.

I put my hand on Taylor's shoulder when I approached, causing him to jump and his wings to flutter with all the chaos of a windmill in a tornado. He turned around, his face one of a frightened puppy, until he realized that it was just me, and his worries were gone.

"Lori!" he cried with affection, wrapping me in a bear hug. "You're awake!"

Tay heard Taylor call my name and wrapped his arms around us too. Then Mothman, with a jealous scree, put his huge arms around all three of us and lifted everyone two feet off the ground.

"Enough!" Drake cried, glaring at Mothman. "Mothman, put them down."

"Scraaaaaawww," cried Mothman, lowering us to the floor in disappointment and sulking away.

Drake turned to me and smiled. "We're glad you're awake, Lori. You should be pleased to know that you weren't out for very long. We carried you up from the house and have been planning our route back to Area 51. The Jacobs are loading up the artifacts as we speak. As soon as they are done, I'll drive you back and get our plans underway." I nodded, and he turned back to his map to finish giving directions to Rachel and Esther. It sounded simple enough.

Tay put an arm around me and I leaned into him and whispered, "What happened to Marie?" His face blanched and he looked to Taylor for guidance. Taylor grimaced and motioned for us to follow him.

"Can we round up Spooky and wait in the car, Drake?" he asked.

"Yes yes, that would be fine," Drake said without looking up from the map. Taylor scooped up Spooky and we followed him to the backseat of the car. I sat between my friends like I always did, with Spooky wriggling from Taylor's arms to nap beneath the steering wheel. The two boys exchanged a glance, then looked to me nervously.

"Marie... well, she... uh..." Taylor stammered, looking for the right words.

"She died, Lori," Tay blurted. The news hit me like a punch to the gut, but I couldn't say I was surprised. With all the monsters crowding Conan's hideout, something bad was bound to happen to someone.

"Oh," I said, "that's awful."

"I know," Tay said, looking down at his feet. "She had a family back home."

I stared at my shoes, wondering what that would be like. Marie had spent the past five years working so hard to aid Drake, working to get her life back, and just as she was about to reach that goal, her life was cut short.

"What happened to you back there, Lori?" Taylor asked. "How'd you get those spells from Conan?"

I explained to them what had happened the best that I could, starting with finally spilling all the details on my dream with Conan. I then had to tell them all about the Winchester Mystery House and how Sarah had given me Conan's old music box, and I told them about my realization of what I had to do on the battle floor. I ended with my talk with Conan about remembrance and grief, and how the stray bullet had somehow struck his ribs.

"We had killed the Hydra by then," Tay mused, running his hands through his hair, thinking hard. "We finally got through its scales by rapid firing at one spot for a really long time. The Jacobs brought some intense guns with them."

"But more wolves came out after that," Taylor said. "We spotted the staircase and made a run for it like you did, but they followed us. Everyone was shooting like crazy. Someone must have misfired and hit Conan without even seeing him."

"I guess that would explain it," I said. I continued to tell them about Conan's final moments, how he had realized that what he was doing was wrong, but how he wouldn't let me save him.

"In the end, I think he was glad someone shot him. I think it's why he finally gave up the spells; dying would give him a new way to search for his family," I said. I blinked back a sudden urge to cry as I thought about the last thing Conan had told me. "He asked if I thought he was going to hell," I said, "and then he asked me to crank the music box for him. He died singing along." I looked at my friends for comfort, their faces concerned. "And then you guys came up."

The sound of the front door popping open interrupted me, and Drake poked his head through the open door. "Lori, if you're feeling well enough, before I send everyone off they would like to know how you got the spells from Conan," he said. I nodded at my friends, and Tay moved out of the way so I could get out of the car. I walked over to the circle of people around the truck and took a deep breath.

"Okay, so a few days ago I had this dream..."

After retelling my story for the second time and answering various questions as best as I could, everyone climbed into their respective cars and began to drive. Spooky sat in my lap this time as we sped down the road, with Mothman rapidly devouring a pear one of the Jacobs had given him.

"Drake?" Taylor said, sounding unsure of himself. Drake raised his eyebrows at us in the rearview mirror.

"Yes, Taylor?" he inquired.

"Will... will we get to go back to our own reality tonight?" he asked. Drake sighed.

"I should think so," he said. He gave an awkward chuckle. "It's hard to believe, children, for the past five years I've been struggling to get out of here, and now... it's just over." He snapped his fingers to demonstrate. "Which reminds me, I should be calling all my other trios. They'll want to be here when we cast the spells. I'm sure they'll be delighted at such news." And with that, he whipped a cell phone out of his pocket, dialed a number, and started talking.

"Guys," Taylor said, sounding nervous again. "What happens to us? I mean, not us, as in everyone, but, you know, *us*?" he said, gesturing to me and Tay and himself. I desperately wanted to know the same thing, but it was going to be a hard question to answer. What would happen to our friendship? Could my fantasy of living in a little San Francisco apartment really come true?

"Well," Tay said, "if I can help it, I'm not letting you guys go." I smiled at him. *So he felt the same way I did.*

"I don't want to lose you two either," I confirmed.

Taylor smiled. "I'd like that. If we could stay in touch somehow. I don't have a cellphone, but I have an email. I can't check it every day, but it works just fine."

Tay laughed. "Wow, I thought I was the only fifteen-year-old in the world without a phone! But yeah, email works great. At least until we can see each other in person again." His face turned serious for a moment. "Wait, we *will* see each other again, won't we?"

I nodded quickly. "Well, yeah! I mean, maybe not until after high school. You guys just live so far." I saw my friends' faces fall, and I quickly added, "But I have email too. And it's only three years. That's not that long."

Taylor sighed. "I guess that's true. It's just... I know we haven't known each other that long, but I'm going to miss you guys."

"I know. Me too," Tay said. I took my friends' hands for a moment and squeezed them tight.

"This isn't goodbye," I reminded them. "We'll find a way to see each other again. I promise."

"Alright," Tay said, squeezing my hand back. "Does anyone have any paper? Let's start exchanging emails." Taylor pulled a notebook out of his backpack and ripped out three pieces of paper and a pencil. We wrote down our emails for each other and exchanged them, but as we were doing so, I could see Drake staring at us in the rearview mirror between phone calls. He looked concerned, like he wanted to tell us something. He opened his mouth for a moment, then closed it, deciding not to tell us whatever he was thinking about. I played the alphabet game with Tay and Taylor after that, and this time we finally found our Z. The game lasted three hours, and by the time we were finished, it was dark outside. We closed our eyes, leaned against each other, and slept.

I was awakened by a sudden bump in the road and a loud mechanical-sounding siren blaring. I looked out the windows at the low, gray, nondescript buildings and desert sand around me. Area 51.

Taylor sat up and peered out the windows too, but Tay didn't wake up until the next speed bump. Drake jerked at the steering wheel, making a sharp turn into a parking lot and causing a sleeping Mothman to slam into the side of his door.

"SCREEE!" he cried in anger and surprise, upset about the violent awakening from his nap. Drake parked the car and turned to look at us, making sure we were all awake. "Follow me," he said, "we're here."

We got out of the car and followed Drake into the building; the very same one where we had started this whole adventure a week ago. Drake led us to the hallway with walls covered in survival gear where we had gotten our backpacks and first met Mothman.

Inside the hall stood three other trios, including the Jacobs, a group of twenty-somethings with heavy black makeup and dyed hair, and three little old ladies. The groups cheered and ran at Drake as soon as they saw him enter the room, assaulting him with a barrage of questions.

He raised both hands in the air, silencing the commotion, and said, "Everyone wait here for a moment, I have some things I need to do in my office." The crowd dispersed with a series of disappointed murmurs. Drake turned to me and said, "Children, you wait here too. Enjoy your time together before everyone else arrives." He bit his lip for a moment, like there was something else he wanted to add, but then he quickly turned away and briskly walked to his office. He shut the door and I could hear the lock turn.

"What was that all about?" Tay asked.

"I don't know, but something's not right," I said. A pang of worry rose in my chest, but I shook my head, shaking the bad emotions from my mind. "Let's just enjoy our time together, like Drake told us to," I said, "we might not get to see each other for a while."

We did try to spend all our time together, despite the fact that it was the middle of the night and we were all still tired from our battles. We strolled up and down the halls and talked. We played twenty questions and I Spy for old time's sake. Taylor found a deck of cards somewhere along the supply wall, and we played the few card games we knew while new trios slowly trickled in the doors to the hallway.

After several more long hours, Drake emerged from his office and declared that everyone was here and that it was time to cast the spells. Everyone cheered.

We followed Drake to a large, high-ceilinged room, not unlike the one we had fought Conan in. On a huge table in the center of the room artifacts were piled several feet high, some of them even spilling out to take up space under the table as well. A little way back there was a podium, where Drake stood solemnly. We gathered around him and he started to speak. He held up a copy of the Voynich manuscript.

"The spells we received from Conan have been derived from his own translations of this ancient manuscript," he said. He then pointed at the table. "And the power required to cast them will come from these universal objects." He cleared his throat, then continued. "A total of four spells must be cast for this to work. They will all take full effect by the time we reach the real layer." Excited whispers reverberated throughout the crowd, but Drake's news only made me nervous. I clutched Tay and Taylor's hands. Spooky anxiously paced around my feet. I heard Mothman's scree-ing somewhere in the background.

Drake cleared his throat yet again, louder this time. "First, a reversal spell. This will send us back to the real layer slowly, by one layer at a time. A second reversal spell will be used to make sure everything stays in its proper layer. That includes all the monsters, ghosts, gods, demons, et cetera that roam this world. When we leave a layer, everything that calls it home will be left behind. That's the real layer for us humans, a pseudo-layer for Mothman, and so on. Make sure you say your goodbyes accordingly."

I turned to look at Mothman, who hovered in the back of the room. I thought of all the times he'd saved our tails: during our fight with the wolves at the Smithsonian, when we almost drowned in the San Francisco Bay, and during out final fight with Conan's monsters. I remembered him flipping over our dinner table just to get to the orange beneath it, and about how much he loved it when Taylor scratched underneath his chin. Mothman might not have been human, but he had been a loving and loyal friend. I was going to miss him.

"The third spell," Drake continued, "will make sure everything appears normal in the real layer. All of these objects here will be transported back to their regular locations, as will all of you. The memories of humans in the real layer will be adjusted accordingly, so that the system of beliefs for determining one's layer of reality will work as it used to." Did that mean that my cousin wouldn't realize I had been missing for a week? Did that mean Mothman could still travel to our layer to visit every once in a while?

Drake drew in a big breath. "The fourth and final spell," he said, "will be a separating charm. It will break your connection with your trio so that you get live independently from one another. You will be able to go farther than a mile from your companions, and your nerves will untangle, so you will no longer be able to feel each other's pain. It also eliminates the risk of the three of you condensing into one person again." Drake surveyed the crowd, his expression one of nervousness, beads of sweat forming on his forehead. He took a shaky breath before starting again.

"However," he said, his voice cracking a little. "The spell is very strong. This is not a reversal spell, but a new spell to negate the effects of the old one. Instead of not being able to get farther than a mile from your companions..." Drake paused, then looked right at me. There was a heavy sadness in his eyes. He looked almost apologetic. "...you will have to stay at least a mile away. It will be physically impossible to get any closer."

A hush fell over the room. My mind went blank with panic. "Email, phone calls, letters, and any other form of communication will not work either," he said. My heart pounded hard and fast in my chest. Did this really mean...?

Drake continued on, confirming our horrible suspicions:

"I'm afraid you will never be able to see each other again."

END

A hush fell over the crowd as we struggled to come to terms with Drake's words. Then a frenzy erupted, with people shouting questions at Drake and rushing to cling to their trios. "ENOUGH!" Drake yelled, calming the chaos. "Everyone meet back here in thirty minutes to start casting the spells. You may take this time to ask questions in a calm and orderly manner and to start saying your goodbyes."

People moved all around me, swarming around Drake and Mothman and other loved ones, but I couldn't bring myself to lift my feet. We could never see each other again? All we'd been through together, and now we'd have to leave each other forever?

I lifted my head to study Tay and Taylor, whose hands I still held. Taylor stared at Drake, shocked from the announcement, tears falling down his cheeks. Tay's face was red with anger.

"All... of that..." he said. "We travel the freaking world together and I can't even write my best friends a damn piece of snail mail." He dropped my hand abruptly and whirled away.

"Tay!" Taylor called. "Tay, come back!"

"I have to go," Tay said, bustling towards the supply hallway. We watched him storm away. My heart was heavy. I faced Taylor, but I felt just like I had the first day I met him: wanting to talk to him, but having no idea how.

"Taylor, I... I..." I stammered. But words wouldn't come; only tears. He held me as I sobbed into his chest, and he cried right along with me.

"I'm sorry," I whispered, "I'm so sorry. I thought we could do it. I-I thought we'd get this little apartment together in San Francisco with Tay and Spooky and Mothman and we could follow our dreams and be happy and—"

"Shhh," he whispered. "It's okay. I wanted us to be happy together too. I wanted that *so* much." He let out a shaky, unstable sigh, the kind you make when you're trying really hard to stop crying. "But I guess we can't have that," he whispered. We stayed in our tear-soaked embrace for a little while longer before I finally pulled away.

"We should probably say goodbye to Mothman and Spooky while we still can. I don't know where they'll end up," I said. Taylor nodded, and together we wandered off to find our moth and our cat.

We spotted Mothman in the corner of the room, hugging Esther and Rachel in each arm. "We'll miss ya, big boy," said Esther. She rubbed his head and he put the women down. They waved at him as they walked away. Taylor and I approached and wrapped our arms around our fuzzy, red-eyed friend. He hugged us back with a gentle "Scraaaaawww."

"Goodbye, Mothman," I said, trying not to get choked up again. "You've been a great friend."

"Thank you for everything, Mothman," Taylor said, rubbing under his chin for one last time. Mothman closed his eyes and purred.

We let go of our friend, sniffling and holding back tears. Someone from another trio held an orange in the air and called to Mothman, and he took off in an instant, swooping down and nabbing the fruit like an eagle after a mouse. Taylor and I laughed for a moment. "Do you think he knows we're leaving him?" I asked.

Taylor's face fell. "I would guess that he doesn't. He seems pretty happy."

Something warm and soft pressed itself into my ankles. I looked down to see my little hairless cat looking back at me.

"Spooky!" I cried, lifting him up into my arms. "Oh, baby, I'm gonna miss you. But you'll be home soon, kitty cat. I hope you like it there." I passed Spooky to Taylor next, who kissed the top of his hairless head. "You're a good kitty. I'm glad you joined us."

"Time to come back!" yelled a voice from the next room. It was Drake, telling us that he was ready. Taylor set down Spooky, and I took his hand. We walked back to Drake's podium to find Tay already there, sitting in front of it with puffy eyes and wet cheeks. We sat down beside him, and I took his hand too. He didn't resist, but he didn't do anything to acknowledge me, either, keeping his eyes steady on the floor.

The rest of the trios crowded into the room, and Drake lit three candles and turned off the lights. He opened the Voynich Manuscript, studied Conan's paper of spells, and began to chant in a strange tongue. As he finished the first spell, a puff of sparkly white smoke rose from the artifact table and evaporated into the air. I assumed that was the power of the special objects being harnessed to fuel the spells. The next two chants proceeded in a similar fashion, another collection of smoke forming after each spell was cast.

When Drake got around to the final spell, I squeezed my friends' hands harder. This was it. There was no going back from here; no way that we'd get to live out the rest of our lives together like I had so badly wanted.

And suddenly the spell was done, quicker than the last three, and the lights came back on and Drake blew out the candles. He looked at his watch.

"It should be about an hour until we're back in the real layer and every spell's effects are complete. This is your last chance to say your goodbyes." And with that, he walked away from the podium.

It's hard to say goodbye when you know for certain it's going to be your last one. What could I say to Tay and Taylor that could explain how I was feeling, how much I was going to miss them, how I felt like I was losing a part of myself? Nothing could put those emotions into words, so we hugged each other and apologized and cried. Tay stayed with us this time, having cooled off from his initial reaction of anger. I couldn't blame him; in so many ways I was angry too.

As we moved back from layer to layer and inched our way closer to home, I started to feel a little better, like a weight was being lifted off my chest bit by bit. Amidst our long goodbyes to each other, we decided we should probably bid farewell to Drake, too. We walked over just as he finished talking with another trio, sending them off with three little plastic-wrapped cylinders.

"Children," he addressed us. We gave him an awkward group hug. "Listen, children, I'm sorry it has to end this way," he said, rubbing the back of his neck. "I know you three were getting close, but—"

"Are you absolutely sure there's no loophole to this?" Tay interrupted. "No way for just the three of us to stay together while everyone else is separated?"

Drake sighed, "Tay, I'm sorry, but—"

"I wouldn't mind the proximity thing," Tay said, "Or the pain. I would even take the risk of becoming one person again." He turned to me and Taylor, "I could put up with all of that if you will."

Taylor smiled, "I could too."

Under different circumstances, perhaps I would have thought about the decision some more, but in that moment all I wanted was my friends. "I will, too. Please, Drake."

"Drake," Tay said, "they're all I want. Please, there has to be something."

"I've never had a family before," Taylor said, "I don't want to lose them."

Family? He considered us a family? Suddenly I longed for our little fantasy apartment ten times more. Yes, we were a family. We could still be a family.

"I'm sorry, children, but there is nothing I can do. There is no 'loophole' like you say. The spell works for everybody or nobody. There is no in between."

My heart dropped and my hope shattered. So it was back to Providence for me after all.

Drake pulled three plastic packages out of his coat pocket, and this time I could tell what they were. Syringes. "Children, this is going to be a hard pain to live with. This experience has been fairly traumatic for a lot of people, and, well..." He handed a packed syringe to each of us, "When I worked for them in the real layer, the government used these to wipe the memories of people who saw things they shouldn't have. If you would like to forget this ever happened, you can." I studied the syringe in my hands, the glass tube filled with a thick, clear-ish liquid.

"Do you mean—" Tay started.

"Inject yourself with that before we get to the real layer and you will have no memory of your time in the pseudo-reality," Drake instructed, "You'll forget everything that you did here and be able to carry on your life as normal." Another trio was approaching, so Drake gave each of us a quick handshake. "Goodbye, children. Thank you for everything you've done." With that, he turned and walked out of my life.

Each of us stared at the needles in our hands, silently debating our options. I knew instantly what I wanted to do. "I'm not using it," I said, "I want to remember you." But as I looked to my friends, I saw that they didn't look as sure and confident as I did. Both boys studied the syringes intensely.

"Taylor?... Tay?" I bit my quivering lip. *We're a family.*

"I want to forget," Tay said suddenly, "if we can't see each other, then I need to forget." His words shook me to my core. Not five minutes before, he was saying that he couldn't bear to live without me, and now he wanted to wipe me from his memory forever.

"Tay, what are you talking about? I thought you loved us," I said.

He met my eyes, and I could see now that he was crying. "I do love you," he said, "but I need to forget. I'm going to be miserable without you because I've been miserable all my life. This week I finally felt like I was worth something, and now I have to go back to the life were no one cares about me and where I'll amount to nothing."

His words stunned me. I had always thought he was happy in San Francisco.

"I've peaked, Lori," he said, "I know what it feels like to be happy now. I know that things are never going to be as good as this again. I need to forget so I don't lose hope for my future."

It broke my heart to hear him talk like that. It broke my heart that I was going to remember someone who would never remember me back. But much like Conan's decision to die, I couldn't change Tay's decision to forget. I hated everything about it, but I couldn't.

"I want to forget, too," Taylor said. I turned to him in shock. My Taylor, my creative, wonder-filled, beautiful-minded Taylor, wanted to forget the adventure of a lifetime?

"Don't tell me you've peaked, too," I whispered, worried about how bad my friends' lives in the foster care system really were.

"No," he said, "well, maybe. I can't tell." He drew in a deep breath. "There's just no wonder left in the world for me, Lori. I understand all the secrets of the universe. There's nothing left to speculate about, no mysteries for me to solve. I love you both, but I don't want to live in a world where I know all the answers." His reason, like every idea that ever came out of his mouth, was poetic and beautiful, but it hurt me all the same. I could feel my heart splitting in two.

"I'm going to miss you guys so much," I said, "and I don't want to forget you. This week has changed me for the better; it's always going to be a part of me."

"We're almost there! Almost home!" Drake called. A cheer went up around the room. I looked around and saw that Mothman was gone. I threw my arms around Tay and Taylor and hugged them as tight as I could. We all started to cry again. "I'll treasure your memory forever," I whispered to the both of them. "Even if you can't remember me back."

"Injections out!" Drake yelled. Tay, Taylor, and about half of the others in the room unpacked their syringes and positioned them against their arms. I looked at Tay and Taylor, my soul shattering as I knew I had less than a minute before I'd lose them forever.

"I love you," I said, "I love you both." They both mouthed an *I love you* back.

"Three!" Drake called.

My heart dropped.

"Two!"

I could see the pain in each of my friends' eyes.

"One!"

I held my breath and tried to be brave.

"NOW!"

Half the room, including my Tay and Taylor, injected themselves with the forgetting syringes. Just as they did, the world flashed white, and everything around me was gone.

*****

I opened my eyes to find myself on the floor of my Grandma's living room, back in my house in Concord. I scrambled to my feet as a flash of memories came flooding back to me. Tay. Taylor. Drake. Conan. The spells. Was this real? Was I home?

I picked up a vase off a shelf and found that it left behind no silhouette of where it had once been. It moved like an object in the real world. I truly was home. I laughed with glee. Drake had done it, he really had.

I heard someone turn the handle on the front door, and suddenly my cousin appeared in the door frame, her face bored and nonchalant. "Hey," she said. "You ready?"

I had briefly forgotten that I was supposed to move in with her. Drake said that everyone's memories in the real layer would be adjusted so they would never know we were gone, but I decided to test that out.

"Um, yeah, my bags are in the kitchen," I said. "By the way, what's today's date?"

"June 16. I have the right pick up date, right?"

"Oh, yeah, you do. I was just checking." That was not the original date she was supposed to pick me up at at all. The spell had changed her memories so that she just thought I was moving in with her later than I should have been.

She rolled her eyes and started towards the kitchen. "Okay, Taylor, I'll help you carry your stuff."

"Actually, I go by Lori now," I blurted. I wasn't sure why I said that. I hadn't been planning to use my nickname from the pseudo-reality in real life, but as I said it, it just felt right. Lori wasn't a name for shallow cheerleaders anymore. It was a name for girls who were brave. It was a badge of honor I had earned from stealing haunted dolls and trapping imps and fighting monster-wolves.

My cousin squinted at me.

"You know, like Tay-LOR," I explained. She rolled her eyes again.

"Whatever. We need to get going." I led her to my luggage, still packed from before I had gone on my accidental adventure. We gathered it up and packed it into the trunk of her car. We opened the doors to the front seats, but as she climbed behind the wheel, my cousin knocked a mug out of the cup holder, causing the lid to pop off and hot tea to spill all over my chair.

"Oh, shit!" She looked at me and her eyes widened. "Oh, dammit, sorry, I meant shoot! Hell, I meant..."

The mess before me faded away and I saw instead a vision of my cousin standing in a bright purple bedroom, the smell of fresh paint invading the air. She stood beside a man I recognized as her husband, and she darted her eyes all around the room.

"Are you *sure* that bookshelf is big enough?" she fretted. "Opal always mentioned how much she loved books. We should have brought up that extra one from the living room."

"Hey, quit worrying so much!" he replied. "It's fine. She'll love it."

She sighed. "I know, I just... she's been through so much. I want her to be happy here."

The vision disappeared and I was back in the present, my cousin still stammering out more expletives and staring at me with worried eyes.

"Hey, um, it's fine, I can sit in the back," I said.

She paused. "You sure?"

I nodded. "Yeah."

She paused again, and then said, "Thanks, Taylor. Lori."

I opened the door to the backseat and buckled my seatbelt. On the chair across from me there was a child's pink car seat, and the window beside it was dotted with the white outlines of stickers that someone had tried and failed to scrape away.

I looked at my cousin, who was finishing wiping up the tea with napkins taken from fast food drive-thrus and stashed in the glove compartment.

"Hey, um," I started, "thanks for doing this. Whatever you have set up for me, I'm sure it's great."

She glanced at me in the rear-view mirror and chuckled. "You know, I think that's just what I needed to hear. It's like you're clairvoyant or something."

I smiled. Somehow, my gift from the Unreal hadn't left me, and maybe that was exactly what it was.

My cousin started the engine, buckled her seatbelt, and drove away from Concord. It wasn't my home anymore, but somehow, I was okay with that.

*****

I didn't notice it until I arrived in my new room in my new house an hour later, but I still wore the jacket I had tried to use to save Conan's life. And inside its pockets were the same things I had been carrying in them in the pseudo-reality: the flip-phone we had used to communicate with Drake and the drawing Taylor had made me. I kept both of them; the drawing was still beautiful, but more importantly, it was drawn by one of my best friends. He didn't remember that had he made it now, nor did he remember the girl in the nurse's uniform and the boy with the guitar, but I remembered him. The drawing gave me hope that somewhere out there Tay and Taylor were following their dreams like I was.

The cellphone still had Drake's number on it, and I would be lying if I said I didn't try to call him, but the calls never went through. However, the phone held one other little memento: a picture taken at night under neon red lighting. A picture of three kids after a long day of exploring Washington, DC. It was the picture we had taken in front of the International Spy Museum and sent to Drake, the one picture Tay, Taylor, and I had taken of the three of us. I looked at the photo every now and then to remind myself that they were real, that everything that had happened to me that one week in June wasn't all in my head. It had been real, and it had mattered.

Life with my cousin's family took some getting used to, as did life at my public school. But eventually, things got better. My cousin and her husband came to tolerate, like, and maybe even love me, as did their preschool-aged daughter. I made new friends at school and got good grades. I came to like my new life just fine, but I never forgot my old one. I still kept some of my Grandma's old things in my room as a reminder of my wonderful childhood with her. I used the inheritance she left me to go to a nursing school in Boston, not San Francisco. I got my degree, and then found a job. I knew that somewhere in an Unreal layer far from mine, she was proud of me.

As my life went on, I made a point to revisit all the locations I had gone on missions to in the pseudo-reality. On a trip to Bridgeport, I convinced my cousin to make a stop at the Warren's Occult Museum. This time I paid an admission ticket and talked with the owner Lorraine. She showed me her basement, including her prized possession, the Annabelle doll. Even though I had seen many of the things in that basement come to life, they weren't so scary anymore. They just reminded me of Tay and Taylor and Mothman, and those thoughts took all my fear away.

On a family vacation to a beach in Rhode Island, my cousin let me take a taxi to Exeter. I relocated Mercy's grave and left behind some flowers and a poem: "Willows weep within the forest/Clouds drift and spin across the sky/Roses grow within the thorn bush/ I wish I hadn't said goodbye." At the top of the paper I had written her words on, I wrote, *In loving memory of Mercy, the world's greatest undiscovered poet.* I proudly left the note and the flowers there for all the world to see.

When I was in college, I took a trip with some friends down to Washington, DC. We saw most of the Smithsonian, but this time no wolves attacked me when I took a peek at the Hope Diamond.

When I had the money I drove myself to St. Louis to revisit the City Museum. I checked for imps behind the exorcist cross and for little ghost girls near the train, but I didn't find any. But I knew that didn't mean they weren't there.

A few years later I caught a flight to California and took a tour of the Winchester Mystery house. We went past Sarah's kitchen, and I caught a glimpse of two pink ceramic bowls in the cupboard. I couldn't help but remember my ice cream and smile.

I drove out to San Francisco on that same trip. I saw Bernard's cell again and took the ferry to Alcatraz both ways, and was pleased to find that this time, it didn't sink. It took quite a bit of driving, but by nightfall I had found Tay's secret apartment rooftop, and I climbed on top of it the way he had taught me to. The city was just as beautiful as I had remembered. I wondered if Tay still came up there sometimes.

I took pictures of all the artifacts we had stolen as yet another reminder that everything that had happened to me was real. It didn't matter if I was the only one who remembered it; it had been real, and I treasured the memories of traveling the country and battling monsters and meeting ghosts with two people who I still considered to be dear, dear friends.

As time went on, I continued to love my job as a nurse, but I had picked up a new hobby along the way. I traveled the world seeing new potentially universal objects and strange places. I took pictures of everywhere I went to, and was always planning something new. Unlike Tay, I never felt like my life ever peaked, and unlike Taylor, I still felt like there was wonder in the world. I never stopped having adventures.

I always knew exactly what to do with myself.

ACKNOWLEDGMENTS

Though I have, in many ways, been preparing to write this novel all my life, it would never have been completed when it was had I not taken a novel writing class my junior year of high school. So first and foremost, a huge thank you to my teacher, Debbie Steiman-Cameron, to the head of University High School, Chuck Webster, for allowing the class to happen. and everyone behind the National Novel Writing Month nonprofit. Another fitting thank you to my classmates, who heard ideas, read samples, and make suggestions: Jordan, Abby, Lauren, Hubert, Kyle, and Eilish. I also want to thank the entire UHS community for their eagerness to support any and every single one of my endeavors, including this one. Thank you to Dean and Pat Toombs and Bill and Leona Elbert, my grandparents, for always encouraging my education. More thank you-s to my family, mom and dad, Garrett and Brooke, Aunt Liz, and all the other aunts, uncles, and cousins. Huge thank you to my first volunteer test readers, Jordan, Eilish, Tom, and Sarah. Thank you to Kaitlyn, Rachel, Allie, and Brookie for listening to my storytelling on our backyard swing set. Thank you my dear friends Sarah, Maren, and Micah. Thank you to my friends from school, many of which have helped me tell stories by taking creative writing classes with me or acting beside me in school plays and musicals; Becca, Amelia, and Jordan; Grant, Jake, Greta, and Jasper; Jack and Brooke; Valerie, Olive, Lauren, and Julia; along with so many wonderful others. More thank yous to my first creative writing teachers, Henry Johnston and Maggie Beckman; my piano teacher Miss Kay, my mentor Jenny Cox, and to Mrs. Ramey and Mrs. Molter, two of the most encouraging and inspirational teachers from my childhood. Finally, thank you to all the people behind Poptropica, Bionicle, Yu-gi-oh, Greek Mythology, and many others for inspiring me to imagine and create.

ABOUT THE AUTHOR

Kellyn Toombs is currently a high school senior at University High School in central Indiana. She has been a storyteller all her life, and this is her first novel and first published work. She hopes to write many more books in the future. She loves knitting, visiting museums, and cuddling with her school's chickens.

Aren't quite ready to leave the world of *The Unreal* behind? Follow the official Tumblr @the-unreal-official to find and share pictures, fan creations, and Q-and-As with the author. Any reviews left on *The Unreal's* amazon.com page would also be greatly appreciated.

Made in the USA
Lexington, KY
25 September 2017